Warriors Inc.

Garth Hobbs

authorHOUSE®

AuthorHouse™
1663 Liberty Drive
Bloomington, IN 47403
www.authorhouse.com
Phone: 1-800-839-8640

First published by AuthorHouse 5/16/2011

ISBN: 978-1-4567-8010-4 (sc)
ISBN: 978-1-4567-8011-1 (e)

Printed in the United States of America

Acknowledgements:

To my (F) Fabulous wife, Tallia, for believing this can be a reality.
To Angela Voges for your invaluable insight and getting this project back on track.
To Gillian and her wonderful enthusiasm for allowing the idea to spring to life in her very bedroom.
To the talented musicians all over the world who's music and lyrics inspired me to do what I love to do.
To my family and friends, this is only the beginning.

Chapter 1

Slimpills

The strangest, most intelligent eyes you will ever see in a human peered over his narrow-based gold glasses.

(Then again, he was a gnome …)

Dr Grumblestumps fumbled around in his little sanctuary, aptly named Gnome Sweet Home. Pictures of relatives, hanging unnoticed, and plenty of books covered the walls. His home wasn't very big, but everything inside had its own place – or that's what Grumblestumps liked to think, anyway. He flicked through his notes and scribbled turbulently with his pencil. He raised his head, interrupted by a hollow knock on his oddly shaped door.

'Do come in,' he intoned.

The visitor swung the door open heavily. After all, the door was half the size of the entire house. This particular house was constructed many hundreds of years ago, by his great-great-great-grand-uncle's father's brother's sister's third cousin twice removed from the town – and then returned, only to confuse the entire population. The town decided to leave him there, and to move the town three clicks and two pennies over.

Inside the new town was a gigantic oak tree with more branches than the local carpenter. Upon closer inspection, the townsfolk found the tree to have pre-dated the town by many hundreds of years. They also noticed that the entire inside of the tree had been hollowed out by the local Armachuck bird that had lived there at about the same time. The newly formed town had the only credible healer and leader at the time, who decided to use the hollow tree and make it the town's very own medical centre and local tavern all in one. Back then, it was thought to be a rather good idea to combine the medical centre and tavern. If you were in any sort of a bar brawl and you lost, you could be attended to without having to travel too far.

Things, of course, had changed since then. The enormous tree had been handed over from one generation to the next, and now belonged to Grumblestumps, serving as a medical centre and home.

The town was very well hidden amongst the kingdom, which had ever so many subdivisions – branched-out towns, cities, mini-cities, forests, caves and swamps, to name a few. It was called Slimpills, and was found beyond the Rocks of Granker, past the Glaciers of Mirror Axels, through the Slush of Kremkin, but just around the corner from the Enslanted Forests of Rottingwood, where all the trees seemed to lean toward the east, no matter where you stood.

Slimpills had its fair share of misadventures, and Rindelrags was one of them.

Doctor Grumblestumps pushed his reading-writing-arithmetic glasses up past his eyes, resting them on his flabby, starred-and-striped, pointed hat. Rindelrags stepped inside.

'I have a problem! I have a problem!' raced out of Rindelrags' mouth.

'Calm down, Rags. What seems to be the matter?' frowned Grumblestumps.

Rags was renowned for his frequent life-threatening diseases.

'Well, you see, Grumble, if I press here wiff me finga, it hurts. And if I press here on me arm wiff me finga, it hurts. Just about everywhere I touch wiff me finga, it hurts. Why, why does it hurt?' whined Rags.

'Aah!' exclaimed the doctor. 'It is very simple.'

Grumblestumps took Rindelrags' finger gently, and eased it up towards his face. He examined it for a while then pushed it back towards Rindelrags' chest.

'It seems to me you have hurt your finger!' announced the doctor.

'Do not worry, Rags. We will have that fixed in no time. Now ... where did I put my hacksaw ...?'

Grumblestumps' logic and knowledge of any medical condition known to man, gnome, troll or faerie had always been impeccable. He did, somehow, tend to forget the simple things in life, like his sanity. Every now and again he'd forget where he put it. From time to time, he'd also forget simply to put it in a jar on top of the fridge, labelled *It's in here!* for emergencies.

Rindelrags looked at Grumblestumps with the most petrified expression on his face.

'Are you going to cut it off?'

Then, his face brightening, 'I suppose I *could* do with one fewer. This one always seems to get in the way of the others, anyway.'

'What?' bellowed Grumblestumps.

3

'Don't be silly, young man! I just need my hacksaw to cut up some of these mushrooms over here.'

Shwarmi mushrooms grew only at night, during the icy winters. They were generally found near the creek that ran through the village. The mushrooms were shaped like the toadstools which were harvested next to the creek. With one exception: these particular mushrooms were blue.

'To rid yourself of pain, Rags, ingest a quarter of these shwarmi mushrooms, soaked in the sap of the crooked elm tree, and mixed with a squeeze of red lemon and a single leaf of crandgrass to hide the sharp taste. Take them twice a day, once at daybreak and once at the first sight of the three moons rising.'

Grumblestumps covered the mushrooms with a neatly woven sack and handed them to Rindelrags.

'You should feel the effects almost immediately ... in around three days, of course. And you may come by again for a check-up, if you wish.'

'Thank you so much, Grumbs,' gushed Rindelrags.

'It's Doctor Grumblestumps. And I bid you good day, Rindelrags.'

Rindelrags waved goodbye as he left through the heavy door. Grumblestumps lowered his reading-writing-arithmetic glasses onto the bridge of his nose, and continued to page through his book, *How to Create Potions with Fewer than Ten Items in a Bag.*

The wind blew silently across the shadows of the trees. Leaves billowed up in the village centre. The sun poked lazy, warm rays through the treetops, greeting the ground below. The town of Slimpills had woken up.

Grumblestumps took his list of things to find and left the house. He was greeted, as always, by Blossom's friendly smile. She was one of the youngest girl gnomes in the village, and preferred to skip everywhere she went. A flower was always in her hand. She loved to wave the flower at everyone who passed by.

'Hi Dr Grumblestumps!' she smiled.

'Morning to you, Blossom. My, what a lovely flower you have this morning!'

'I found it next to the stream!' she exclaimed happily.

'May I have a closer look?' he asked.

She smiled up at Grumblestumps and handed him the flower. He peered at it intently. She turned, and started to skip down the path.

'Wait, Blossom – do you not want this back?' he asked quickly.

'No, thank you. There are many more over by the stream. Besides, I am off to play now.'

Grumblestumps found the flower to be very unusual for this part of the kingdom. He decided to go and look for himself. Approaching the stream, near the wooden bridge, he saw that a huge bunch of the flowers had started to grow. The bridge creaked as he crossed it heavily. He walked up to the flowers and knelt down. A subtle smell ... beeswax and ginger.

He grabbed a fistful of the yellow-and-green flowers and shoved them into the leather bag hanging from his waist. For some odd reason, the flower's name would not come to him. This baffled him.

He felt a tap on his shoulder, and turned around, pushing his glasses up towards his eyes.

'Oh. It's you,' he said drily.

'Morning to you too, Grumblestumps,' Snork retorted.

'I find it strange to see you on this side of the stream,' replied Grumblestumps.

Snork was a local gnome who loved getting his nose into everyone's business. He wore a blue. pointed hat, tilted to one side. It had a badge half-sewn onto the front that read *Everyone's business is good business.* Snork ran a gossip newspaper, which seemed to do rather well in this part of the woods. He always seemed to find stories worth gossiping about.

Grumblestumps had never liked him. Especially since he only believed in hard facts. Facts you would come across in books.

'Well, it's a nice morning to be walking around,' replied Snork, glancing over his shoulder.

Grumblestumps noticed how uneasy he looked.

'Waiting for, or running away from, someone, Snork?'

'No, no,' said Snork, fidgeting.

'Then why the constant checking behind you?' asked Grumblestumps.

'I ... I was just trying to remember which way led back to the village. As you know, I don't normally find myself in these ... er ... parts.'

'Well, I guess you'd better get going, then. Before a Jagged-Claw Wolf finds you.'

Snork turned pale. He swallowed loudly.

'I didn't know they lived around these parts.'

Grumblestumps laughed.

'They don't! But I am sure you would love to make a story out of that.'

Snork pondered the fact for a moment, then smiled.

'Yes! Yes! I could call it *Hungry Beast Out for Revenge.* Or even, *Beast or Demon? The Phantom that Haunts our Woods.*'

Grumblestumps smirked and clapped his hands.

'A tad extreme, Snork, but, if you must, I might just find myself reading the rest of the story.'

Snork nodded, waved, and toddled away into the woods.

From a distance, a lazy mist crept towards him.

Grumblestumps felt the hairs on his neck stand up. He looked towards the mist and within a split second, four shadows fitted through the light among the trees. They were too far away to run towards, at his age. Snork had disappeared very quickly too ... Deep in thought, he wandered off back towards the village.

Twigs creaked and snapped underfoot as he walked. A light flickered in the corner of his eye. He stopped, and turned towards it. A ray of light filtered through the trees and bathed a bush, which was densely covered with leaves. The bush seemed ... ominous. He knelt down and picked up the shiny item that lay beside the bush. It was a piece of crooked glass, shaped like a dragon's claw. It had writing on it, which Grublestumps read carefully:

Four carries Five.

Puzzled, he placed the object carefully in his pocket.

The town of Slimpills was in full swing by the time Grumblestumps got back. A clamour of voices wafted cheerily through the air, yet the morning troubled him. The back of his short neck still prickled, as if a Yellow-Pin Spider had clamped down on his flesh. A bellow interrupted his thoughts from across the main street.

'A *very* good morning to you, Doctor Stumps!'

Rifflerack was a stout fellow, a little shorter than Grumblestumps and much younger. He had a beaming smile that covered the whole of his face. His long sideburns hugged his cheeks. A yellow jacket covered up a white shirt, which was neatly tucked into his brown pants.

'I have something for you. It came just this morning!' he said.

'What is it, then?' asked Grumblestumps, walking over to meet Rifflerack halfway down the street. The sun had come out vibrantly and warmed everyone's moods. Rifflerack pulled out a parchment from a satchel that hung from his shoulder. It was tied up efficiently by a thread, gold in colour. The note gleamed with importance. And Grumblestumps knew it. Even the wind seemed to hold its breath as he took the parchment from Rifflerack.

'It arrived very early this morning.'

'Oh?' questioned Grumble.

'Yes. It took me at least six bells to realise it had arrived at all.'

Many years ago, the king and queen realised that if they wanted to communicate effectively with their subjects, they had to find a way that everyone would understand. They were simple human beings, lacking magic, and relied upon conventional methods. A wise old man and several of his retired friends came up with the idea of reverting to the old system, which had been trusted for so many years. The only problem was that the system was terribly slow, becoming slower as the people who ran it slowed with age and time.

Enter Arrow Mail – a simple process that delivered messages very quickly. More quickly, at least, than a bunch of old men trying to climb a staircase one stair at a time.

If the king and queen needed to send an extremely important message across the kingdom, they would take a parchment made out of Rotting wood and write their message on it with a Wallow-shriek Bird's tail feather. They would seal it with a special golden thread, and hand it down to a Sender. A Sender was an archer who could ride a stallion and shoot a bow and arrow at the same time with great accuracy. The Sender would ride to a designated point, on the outskirts of each village in the kingdom. The points were considered safe havens for anyone to pass through. The Royal Throne swore that if anyone came to any harm at these points, the offender would have something taken from him. Like his life.

Each point was clearly marked with a sign, on which hung the name of the town or village. Next to the sign hung a round, wooden target, marked with black and white stripes. It would sway at a generous height above the ground from a tree. Written clearly in black on the target, was:

Insert Arrow Here.

The Sender would slide an arrow through the rolled-up parchment, gallop towards the target, and take aim carefully. He would shoot the target, never daring to miss. The Senders trained every day, since they could carry only one arrow to hit the target. As it was said in the kingdom, if they missed, they would be sorely missed. No Sender had ever failed his duty.

A rope attached to the board would pull and stretch along several wooden spikes that kept it up above the ground. The maze of rope ran for a fair distance before it came to a sudden end, and to a bell. When an arrow hit the target, the target's movement would tug on the rope and cause the bell to ring – about seven times, before the movement in the system was lost and the bell fell silent.

'Six rings, you say?' asked Grumblestumps.

'Yes! I was almost too late. But to this day, not one mail missed,' Rifflerack continued proudly.

Grumblestumps smiled and gazed into the distance. He was still very distracted. He had never liked distractions. Still puzzled, he held the parchment up to the sky and stared

9

at it for a while. Sure, Arrow Mail came to these parts every so often – but never bound with a gold thread.

'Do you see this over here?' pointed Grumblestumps.

'I think so,' said Rifflerack, seeing nothing but not wanting to sound silly.

Grumblestumps pointed to the edges of the stitching, which meandered in a messy crisscross fashion through the parchment.

'If you look closely, you can make out a hidden message.'

'A hidden message?' asked Rifflerack nervously.

'Yes!' replied Grumblestumps, enthusiastically.

'Why would anyone want to hide a message within a message?'

'To conceal a secret from all but a few people, or a single person ...' mused Grumblestumps.

'Thank you for bringing the message to me, Rifflerack. I must be off now to see if I can decipher this message quickly. It may be of great importance. Nobody would go to so much trouble for us to hear what the weather's like in the Slush of Kremkin.'

'Slushy?' said Rifflerack hesitantly.

'Oh – and not one word about this to anyone. At least not till I have had a look at it.'

Grumblestumps patted Rifflerack on the back and walked off towards his home.

The morning had stretched out all of its limbs, and pushed the rest of the day above its head nicely.

Chapter 2

Silvercrown

Beneath the lush forest canopy lay magical Silvercrown, a hidden village of faeries. Here, the light magically reflected off the dewdrops caught on the moss. Lit candles hung from overgrown leaves. The light danced off the pathways between the trees that hugged the village. It gave a sense of ever-glowing life that made those who found themselves there proud. And those who lived there were very proud to be known as the Silvercrown faeries.

Silvercrown faeries were special in their own right – they were the only faeries to allow parties after midnight and to be able to throw anyone who misbehaved out of the village.

Including the Head of the village.

When the village was first formed, the Head of the village had always been an influential figure. It was someone who had experience, whom the village could always look up to. Over time, the honour of being the Head was handed down from generation to generation. And so it fell upon a stout fellow named Stirron.

Stirron had done much in his lifetime, and had seen the highs and lows of faerie life. Many of the village faeries simply considered him lucky. They thought his experience came to him through a vision, or by the post. Others just thought he was too lazy to go anywhere, that he waited for heroes to return with their stories, to die in later battles and to leave those stories to Stirron to retell as his own. And others never seemed to catch on to the idea that he was the village Head, being as short as he was.

So not being physically able to stand up to the name, a new name was born. He became the Headling, half a head in size. Stirron was strong-willed and arrogant, with a round head that could be mistaken for a toadstool.

This particular morning was no different to any other in Silvercrown. The sun slowly raised its long, warm hands to touch the far end of the village. Rays flickered through the early mist and shadows started to creep from the ground. The early chirps of Tweedle Birds rang in the branches above, helped along by the light breeze blowing gently through the sleepy village.

'Oww, my head hurts!'

Kasandra's words were muffled through a yellow and pink quilt that was two sizes too big for the bed. The quilt had pictures of hearts and roses stitched into blocks. The blocks formed a pattern that resembled a very badly designed chess board, made by someone who was colour blind. With a limp. As Kasandra peered over the quilt, the sun's rays decided to pop into the room. She blinked, rolled over, and threw the blankets back over her head. She lay very still, not daring to move a muscle in case her muscles discovered that they were still sore from the night before. The smell of freshly picked roses drifted through the window. A door creaked open and footsteps stumbled into the room.

'You'd better get up, or your breakfast will get cold.'

Prince was a young and faithful faerie who had managed to calm Kasandra in her wild days. Well, to a certain degree, anyway. Kasandra had always been the first one at every party, and always the last to leave. So much so that she would sometimes still be there when the next party started. Kasandra was the first woman to qualify as a warrior faerie, and had always been inspired to follow in her father's footsteps.

Some would say that Prince and Kasandra made a very odd couple, like combining dragon's tooth and tumbleweed as an antidote for heartburn. Both pairings work, in an odd, disjointed kind of way. Prince liked to enjoy simple things in life – sitting by the fire and stirring it with a stick, long walks through the misty forest at dusk. Kasandra had just wanted to get sloshed at the after-hours pub and take some hunk home for a one-night stand, until she met Prince. A great deal of her wildness remained, this being simply who she was.

She sat up and threw her legs over the side of the bed. There were holes in her tights, and a big tear in one of her sleeves. She pushed her hair out of her face and rubbed her bloodshot eyes. She still had sticky marks on her cheeks from where she'd fallen face-down into a plate of sugar pies. Slowly, she got to her feet and walked over to a mirror that lay on the crooked wooden table, which also bore her heavy, broad-edged sword and helmet. She picked up the mirror and stared into it for a long time, then flashed a smile like a lit-up diamond mine. 'Yup, I've still got it!' she remarked. 'How can anyone resist a smile like mine?'

Confidently, she strode to the bedroom door that had little knot holes in it that one could peer through if one really tried. She pushed it open and stomped heavily into the next room.

A rectangular table with awkward legs dominated the room. The legs looked as if they could be made of miniature unicorns sticking out from every angle, yet when one looked at them carefully, one saw an overgrown thorn-bush instead. In a corner across the room was a rocking chair and a half-completed quilt. At the other side of the room stood a huge stone fireplace, where flames danced excitedly. A black iron pot hung in the fire, looking as if it was just there for some company. Above the table hung a tremendously oversized chandelier that seemed to wonder how it got there in the first place. The chandelier was a wedding gift from Prince's parents, who always seemed to think that their Prince could have done better in selecting his life partner. Prince was an honest chap, with a simple mind. He was a simple man to please too. Knowing that Kasandra would always come back to where life was comfortable was all he needed to know. The chandelier hung proudly above the unicorn table and glowed softly as the morning started to bare its light. Their home had few valuables, but life was good within it – or so it seemed for our young Prince.

Kasandra walked over to the rocking chair and grabbed the half-finished quilt. She threw it over her shoulders and walked over to the fireplace to warm up.

'Um ... Honey Pie, I am not finished with that one yet,' said Prince softly.

Kasandra stood dead still and stared at the fire as if she was mesmerised.

Prince decided to break the spell and asked, 'Are you in the mood for any breakfast this morning?'

She turned around and gazed at him for a while, then smiled.

'Of course, darling. I am. Thanks for being so thoughtful again.'

She walked over to him and ran her fingers through his hair, which made him smile for a moment. She sat down where a place was set for her on the table and looked down to see what was prepared. It did not take too long before she dived into her food like a pig into mud, and the sausages were slapping into her throat like seal that had an itch on its back. Or maybe there was a hole in her stomach to fill.

She looked up and asked with a mouth full of meat, 'These are pretty good sausages. Where'd you get them?'

Prince wiped off the bits of outspoken sausage off his face and replied, 'These I got from Windell, our butcher, across town. I know it's a way down, but certainly worth the effort, were these sausages! I will take a walk down anytime, if it gets you to eat them like that!'

He pointed to the empty plate that was full a few seconds ago.

She wiped her mouth on her sleeve and rose up from her chair.She leaned over and kissed Prince on the forehead to thank him for a wonderful breakfast. She turned and walked over to her room to freshen up, sniffing her armpits along the way.

In the town centre, faeries were gathering already for the day's work. Some had set up their stalls, and others were chatting about the previous night's festivities. The blacksmith's hut stood across from the baker's. He'd become renowned for his skill in making exceptional weaponry. His speciality, of course, was his ability to make any blade to suit anybody's needs. However, some thought he had gone a bit mad when they saw the sword he'd presented for their fearless Kasandra.

Morgin the Blacksmith was a tall, strong fellow, with

arms the size of oversized rocks that were tied up in a sack; every muscle urged its way out of his shirt. His head gleamed in the sunshine as the light caught hold of the sweat above his brow. He wore an apron around his square waist, which gleamed in shades of black.

'Top of the morning to ya!' said Morgin to a senior faerie who walked by.

'Expect a visit soon from the Headling,' remarked the senior as he shuffled past.

Morgin thought this was an odd thing to say, but continued to bash a very hot piece of iron. Soon enough, rumours flew around the town. Some said that the sky was falling; others that war was looming. Still others laughed it off as a practical joke doing another round. Not long before the sun was up at its best, an urgent announcement ran through the village that asked all the faeries to gather in front of the blacksmith. Morgin thought this was an outlandish request, but knew that soon enough light would be shed on the subject. It did not take the faeries long to gather in front of the blacksmith, as everyone felt the excitement in the air. The more senior faeries had their doubts, since they were the ones that had seen worse in the past. Something had to be wrong. Why would the Headling call a town meeting on such short notice? More importantly, why was the meeting not at the town hall?

As everyone gathered and waited patiently, a commotion was heard from down the dusty path that led out towards the forest. In the distance, they saw what looked like the Headling, surrounded by senior faeries who were all talking at the same time. The senior faeries were shoving each other out the way to have their chance with the Headling. Stirron and the seniors started to approach the crowd, urging them to make way for them to pass. The crowd heard their mumbles as they walked by.

'Who do we send?'

'Our reputation is at stake.'

'We don't want to be embarrassed.'

Stirron walked over to the hut and saw Morgin standing with his huge hammer swung over his shoulder. Stirron extended his hand to Morgin. They smiled at each other.

'Do you have anything big enough for me to stand on?' Stirron asked.

Morgin mumbled, then pointed to his anvil. Stirron frowned with his one long eyebrow. Before Stirron could object, Morgin picked him up and planted him onto the anvil with a thunk. The Headling dusted himself off and smiled at the restless crowd. He raised his hands and said, 'Now, now ... please, calm down. Thank you. I am sure there are many questions to be asked.'

From the back of the crowd, an elder shouted, 'Can you tell us what on earth is going on?'

'Yes, yes. In a minute. But first, if I can just have everyone's attention for a moment, and please settle down!' Stirron replied.

'Rumours have been floating around, which are all untrue. I have asked you all to gather today to tell you that in the early hours of this morning, the queen was attacked!'

Some in the crowd gasped. A lady faerie screamed in shock.

'Please! Calm down!' said Stirron, again.

'The queen was attacked by five beings who forced their way into the castle. They also forced the queen to give up that which keeps this kingdom and sanctuary we all live in, alive.'

Stirron paused in the silence.

'I am afraid the queen has lost her marbles.'

The faeries looked on in disbelief.

Stirron continued, 'The time has now come to relay some exciting news. The queen has sent a message to all the villages in the kingdom. She is desperately seeking someone who is brave enough to find these fiends and bring them to justice. Word has been received that this act was perpetrated by goblins.'

'Now, hold on a minute!' said Morgin. 'What has this got to do with us? I mean, by the sounds of things, those menaces seemed to know what they were doing. How did they get past all the guards? And why is the queen asking us?'

'As proud Headling,' replied Stirron, 'it's my honour to announce that we will soon be sending someone to represent us in the quest to find her majesty's missing marbles.'

'That's all good and well,' retorted Morgin, 'but how do we know who to send? All our fighters have gone, and those who stayed are too old to fight. Any others who show some promise are too young to send to their deaths!'

Another loud scream issued from the lady in the crowd.

Morgin added quickly, 'I mean, to send ... well ... you know what I mean ...'

Back at home, Kasandra was getting herself ready for the best start to her day. She grabbed her shiny broad-edged sword. It gleamed in the morning sun, and reflected her face. The sword was made of the finest iron money could buy. The handle was a combination of iron and lava rock, which prevented it from separating from the blade during battle. The blade itself was as sharp as blades could be made. The sheath was made out of dragon hide. Kasandra swung the sword over her shoulder, tying the sheath around one side of her shoulder and under her arm, so it could be buckled around the chest.

She picked up her helmet and shoved it onto her head. Prince always thought the helmet was too big for her, but would not argue with her. The helmet had belonged to her father, one of the most successful warriors that Silvercrown had ever known. She always wore it with pride, and vowed that one day she would walk in his footsteps with his helmet held high. Many in the village doubted this, even more so because she was a woman. She fought these doubts with her tenacity, her willingness to train hard, and her eagerness to prove them wrong, fuelled by the lack of sheer love and respect from her father who never believed in her.

The bedroom door opened. Prince's head popped in, and he smiled at her.

'So, are you off to conquer the kingdom for a change, or just the kingdom at the bar?' he asked.

'Very funny,' she replied. 'I thought I would do some training today. Feeling a bit motivated this morning – must have been those dreadful sausages,' she added with a wink.

'Good thing you're going to practise. I just recently put up the new targets and fresh straw dummies for you to practise on. I even painted evil faces this time, and not the usual smiley ones that always irk you so much.'

Kasandra walked over to Prince and pinched his cheek.

'Did I ever say how much you mean to me?'

'No – and let's keep it that way!' he joked.

She strolled out the door, beaming.

Around the side of the house lay an arena that was cordoned off by a wooden fence. The fence was made of logs the size of ogre legs. Straw covered the arena floor; dummies and targets lay in wait for their next pummelling. Kassandra eagerly jumped the fence, catching her leg on one of the poles. She dropped face-first into the straw. With one quick movement, as if it were rehearsed, she rolled over, got to her feet and pulled out her sword, ready to duel.

The straw dummies' menacing faces excited her immensely. One was painted with broken teeth and an eye patch. Another was done up with a knife between its teeth. The last one, however, bore the words *You don't look so tough, Missy!* in big, black letters.

Three small daggers in the strap of her sword-sheath glittered in the morning sun. She grabbed all three in a flash. Before the straw dummy could bat an eyelid or eye-patch, its eyes and mouth were replaced by precisely thrown daggers. She dived across the ground, rolled to the next victim, and stabbed it with her sword. With the sword still quivering in the dummy's stomach, she got up, dusted the straw off her leather blouse and brushed the hair out of her face. She then dived again, rolling over to a bale of straw that she grabbed with both hands and flung across the arena. It hit the last dummy standing. Straw exploded everywhere. 'Excellent!' she yelled gleefully. She turned to fetch her sword, and saw Prince running towards her.

'Kasandra, you need to come quickly! The Headling is holding a very urgent town meeting and needs everybody to be there. That includes you!'

Kasandra frowned. 'Wasn't I chased out of the last meeting?'

'Well, yes, but only because you were drunk and threatened to cut the Headling up real nice,' said Prince.

'I did not threaten him! I merely told him I would cut him a new ... well ... you know ...'

'That doesn't matter now. You are needed at the meeting this minute!'

She stared at Prince. 'Well, if it's that important, I'd better go.'

Prince added, 'Quickly too, they are expecting you. Oh, would you mind just brushing your hair before you leave?'

Kasandra took her hidden dagger out of one of her boots, and ran it a few times through her hair. She picked up and sheathed her gleaming sword. Turning to Prince, she blew him a moist kiss and moved towards the village.

The discussion seemed to carry on for quite some time before anybody noticed that the subject of their discussion had arrived. She stood with her arms folded, listening to the commotion intently.

'I might add that if we choose someone as noble and courageous as the one we have chosen, it will not only bring great honour to our village, but great wealth too,' Stirron was saying.

'You never said anything about wealth?' another elder shouted.

'Well, no, I didn't mean wealth as in money, I meant wealth in that our village will be acknowledged by the queen herself, and that we will be held in high regard by the other parts of the kingdom that surround us.'

A voice in the crowd raised itself above the rest.

'Then who do you propose we send to help in this conquest?'

'Oh, that would be you!' said Stirron.

The crowd turned and stared in the direction from which the voice had come.

'Me? Why me?' questioned Kasandra. 'Surely you are looking for someone with more … er … manliness than I would be able to bring to the task?'

'That's exactly why we chose you. We need someone who is not afraid to take to battle, no matter what,' added Stirron. 'We feel that you are the only one left in our village with nothing to lose. Someone who can make this village proud, and prove to us all that she is the warrior her father once was.'

Kasandra thought about Stirron's words. She frowned about them too. She wasn't quite sure what to think, but thought about it anyway. She weighed up the idea of succeeding in this conquest, considering how she would be seen in a new light – a light which would not shine on her drunken and rebellious ways, but on what made her who she was.

'Any objections to this selection? May we have a quick vote – all in favour of Kasandra?' said Stirron.

Everyone except Kasandra raised their hands. She smirked, rather enjoying the fact that it was her or no one.

'Are you sure you are ready for this?' Prince asked, nervously. He was trying to fold some of her clean, pressed shirts. He slipped past her and gently put her clothing on the bed.

'They said to pack light, darling,' commented Kasandra.

'I know, but I just want you to look your best. You know, best shirt forward, or is it best boot?'

'Yeah, yeah, something like that. Now move over.'

She moved towards the side table that hugged the creaky wooden bed, and grabbed her sharpening stone.

'I'll be needing this.'

Prince decided to look the other way, pretending he didn't hear her. As much as he loved her, there were moments in his life in which he wished he'd married someone who didn't find such satisfaction in slitting new holes in people's clothing, just because they happened to look strangely at her. However, he knew that with her on his side, he would never, and he meant *never*, lose a fight. No matter how merry she would get.

Kasandra grabbed her backpack and swung it over her shoulder. She hung her sword over the middle of her back and put the daggers in the front of her belt that kept the sheath in place. Finally, she placed her helmet carefully on her head. It slipped forwards and momentarily covered her eyes. With a flick of her right hand, she moved it back into place. The helmet *was* a little bit big. Morgin the blacksmith did offer to resize it for her, but she insisted she would grow into it. The helmet meant a tremendous amount to her. She ensured her father that in his last days, she would wear it at all times, especially when she went to battle. When she put the helmet onto her plaited hair, she was certainly in the mood to make someone aware of how much they loved their family and possibly their crown jewels.

Kassandra leaned over to Prince and looked him firmly in the eye.

'I will be back before you know it.'

A tear crossed Prince's cheek. He forced a smile and nodded.

'I will miss you too.'

She ruffled his hair, then hugged him tightly before walking away.

'Why walk when you can fly?'

She stood still, allowing her wings to stretch, then looked up at the sky. She pushed gently off the forest floor.

Prince waved goodbye and slowly closed the door behind him.

'Ouch'

Looking down, he noticed he'd closed the door on his foot.

Chapter 3

The Palace Of Elders

The sun rose early to the chirps of the blue-breasted birds that proudly displayed bright red rings circling their necks. Chirpers seemed to live happily in this particular neck of woods. These woods were not your average set of woods, as they barely grew above the huge stone buildings that surrounded them. Its trees seemed to dwell within the walls – and the very community – of wizards at the Palace of Elders. The Palace of Elders was the biggest and oldest part of the kingdom. The wizards proudly boasted about this fact. Since these walls were the first to be built, they felt that the wizards should be first at everything.

They were even first in line to receive their yearly snifflings, granted by the queen since she took First Chair. The wizard elders did not accept gracefully the fact she was able to retain the name First Chair, when they knew, or at least liked to think, that the First Chair had always remained in their palace, next to the fire that never stopped burning in the lounge above the dining room. Wizards who lived in the Palace were generally cold people. Well, at least most people thought so. Although some thought that these 'old men' were rather sweet – cold, but sweet. Others suggested the wizards were just slow.

Jargo took a sip from his cup of fermented tea and stared across the room for a moment. Jargo was one of the youngest wizards to retire to the Palace of Elders. He decided early one morning that he had had enough of trying to save the kingdom from blowing itself up for the thirteenth time. He liked to think that it mostly seemed worthwhile, until the day on which trying to save the kingdom had cost him his favourite cloak. He decided from that day on that he would become grumpy like the rest of the elders who lived peacefully within the Palace walls.

'They called us slow *again*?' asked Jargo.

'It seems so, but what do those ogres know anyway?' replied Mezzar.

'They're just looking for another fight. And somehow I just don't think they understand that if they wish to try, their whole village will vanish again.'

Jargo smiled.

'I see Grenger loves that spell all too much!'

'Can you pass on a sweet root cookie, please?' asked Jargo.

Mezzar slowly walked over to the table where the cookies lay and handed one to Jargo. He turned and strolled over to the fire, which had been pushing its warmth into the room intently. Mezzar was one of the elders who had served on the council for a few years. The council consisted of six very senior members of the wizard community. Mezzar's position on the council involved looking after foreign affairs. Luckily, not many affairs were happening among wizards, as most of them were too plain old to bother. However, he had to make sure that the community was kept pure as possible, and the council felt that its trade secrets were best kept to itself.

Jargo had decided in his early years of retirement that he should take up a hobby of some sort. Human magic had intrigued him for many years, and he decided to give it a bash.

He pointed out, 'You know, Mezzar, I thought this human magic would be far easier, but I find it often difficult to stuff things up my sleeve.'

Mezzar nodded and replied, 'Maybe you should get longer sleeves.'

Jargo added, 'Or shorter arms.'

'Maybe you should stick to the more conventional magic, called wizardry.' said Mezzar. 'Somehow, I do not think that the council approves of your doings with this so-called magic. They believe it is a mockery of its origins in wizardry.'

Jargo pondered and said, 'Or maybe they are just jealous.'

'You know, I am getting rather good at it, if I may say so myself,' beamed Jargo.

Mezzar replied, 'Good that you think so.'

'Well, I do have a trick for you, if you are interested. I learnt this one only recently.'

'No thank you, leave that one for the children whom you are expected to entertain later today.'

'Oh, that's right! I nearly forgot about that. Thanks!'

Jargo took another sip of his tea and began to smile.

Bang!

He looked up from his cup of tea, and gazed at the source of the noise. The head of the council, Grenger, had appeared out of nowhere. Some wizards tended to appear out of nowhere, especially if they were late for breakfast. Grenger walked over to the breakfast table and helped himself to moss-covered toast and freshly ground tree-nuts. With a half a mouthful of toast, he mumbled a 'Good morning!' to everyone in the room.

One of the other elders was standing nearby. With much annoyance, he wiped some of the toast that had flown out of Grenger's mouth from his robe.

'I trust that it is a good morning for all, as I received some very good news during the course of last night.'

Not everyone at the Palace of Elders liked to receive good news. Some preferred not to receive any news at all. News meant that they might have to get up and do something. Some elders in the Palace were very particular about their daily approach to what was left of their lives. So, anything out of the ordinary was just not allowed. Others were quite happy to sit out their remaining time at the Palace doing absolutely nothing, since that is what the kingdom owed them anyway.

'Does it concern us all?' asked Mezzar. One of the elders who had just taken a bite out of his morning biscuit almost choked when he heard that question. He was hoping that this was not going to ruin what looked like a perfectly good breakfast.

'Well, it depends,' said Grenger, 'on whom we classify as all.'

Mezzar frowned and said, 'I suppose the council will decide on this, no doubt?'

'Yes.'

'Oh,' replied Mezzar uncertainly.

Jargo continued to search in his robe for the trick that was meant to come out about ten minutes ago. He sat there with his right arm half way down his robe, which came fiddling out between his legs.

'I found it!' he said gleefully, before falling from his chair and onto his face.

The others turned and shook their heads disapprovingly.

'I think the council will meet within the hour to discuss the matter,' said Grenger. 'And Mezzar, will you please ensure that the other four elders are informed?'

'I will inform them immediately.'

'Good. I will see you in my chambers in a bit.'

Bang!

There was a slight trail of dust as he left the room.

It was nearly twelve o'clock when Jargo found himself scratching in the trunk that he kept under his bed.

'Oh gosh, I am going to be late.' he mumbled.

He was searching for a deck of cards that he needed for the first magic trick he wanted to use on the children. As a general rule within the Palace, once a wizard retires to the comfort of being able to get old without having to slay an ogre just after lunch, it was expected that he spend at least three sessions a week with the children, sharing his experiences. This was to help prepare the young ones to become full-time wizards. Wizards only ever intervened in situations when it was absolutely necessary – and, more importantly, when it did not conflict with any meals. Food seemed very important to them; it was the only thing that seemed to give them satisfaction. Anything else just seemed to be a waste of time.

He had pushed the bed away from the corner of the room and put on its side, so that he could take a better look what was underneath it. To his surprise, he had found a few more things he thought had gone missing, even his favourite cup. He'd blamed its disappearance on the last visit he had to contend with from his great aunt, who didn't seem to like him very much.

He looked again at his watch, which hung elegantly from a silver chain. It was tied to his dark leather-studded belt, which he'd picked up at a bazaar when it was marked down to half-price. He saw that he had two minutes to get where he was supposed to be.

He stood up from the floor and took out his wand. The wand was made out of wood that came from the deepest parts of the Enslanted Forests of Rottingwood. The trees there looked like spiral staircases, and had been there for a very long time. His wand's spiral grooves created shadows that made the wood look like it was different shades of brown. He turned and pointed the wand towards the middle of the floor.

'Expose yourself!' he yelled, and a collection of sparks flew out from the tip of the wand. They circled the room a few times before they disappeared. Out of nowhere, a book with golden markings landed on the floor with a loud thud.

He leaned down, picked the book up from the floor and dusted it off.

'*One Hundred and One Ways to Grow a Beard*?' questioned Jargo.

It opened slowly, exposing a deck of cards where the pages should have been.

'Right,' said Jargo. 'As if I was ever going to read this book again.'

The cards quickly found their way into the pouch Jargo kept tied to his studded belt. Without hesitation, he moved outside and stood still for a moment. Using real wizardry did have its benefits. Sometimes life was simply too inconvenient not to use it. Now was one such time.

Jargo spun around and flicked his wand.

He politely said 'Places I want to be!', then vanished, leaving a puff of dust behind.

A mouse, hiding in the grass nearby, coughed.

The children played quietly in the park in the middle of the Palace. Here, trees found themselves growing very happily on the banks of the small brook that waved itself past. Birds buried their nests between the branches that swayed in the light breeze. In the shade of these trees was an iron bench that resembled the criss-cross of some wizard's old grandmother's stitching. The sun was beaming down from a perfect blue sky and warming the smile of every flower that looked towards it.

Bang!

Jargo looked down at his robe and lightly dusted it off.

'Alright, children, let's all gather over there at the bench,' Jargo instructed, pointing towards the trees.

The children gathered excitedly. They seemed to like him far more than the usual wizards that came for their weekly sit-down. They found him far more interesting, as he never really wanted to discuss his experiences with them. They always expected him to do something really funny. Maybe Jargo never intended this; he was just pleased that they would remember the times he spent with them. Amazingly, he could never remember much of what was told to him in his day, and he vowed that when it was his turn, something would stick in the children's minds for them to use, even if it was just a human magic trick. He liked trying the tricks on the children, even if they never worked properly.

'Afternoon, everyone. Today, I am certain that I have one that is going to work!' he proclaimed proudly, while rolling up his sleeves. A laughing murmur rippled through the group of youngsters, which Jargo quickly hushed.

'Can anyone tell me what we did last time we met?' he

asked. A young boy, who always sat in the middle in the front, raised his hand.

'Didn't you burn your hat last time?' he said, with uncertainty.

'Well, besides that. What else can you remember?'

Another hand popped up from a slightly older boy in small, black-framed spectacles.

'Didn't you also tie your hands so tightly together that we had to call someone to help you get the knot undone?'

'Well, that too...,' hesitated Jargo, 'but can anyone remember what we *really* learnt that day?'

'I think we all learnt that if you do not prepare properly, you are sure to get yourself tied in a knot!' a voice noted from the back of the group.

Jargo nodded and added, 'Good, good. Now, I am certain I have got this trick down to a fine art!'

All the boys turned to each other and started to snicker so violently that they all collapsed in a heap as if they were hit by an earthquake.

'Now, now! That's enough! I am sure today will be the day you will remember for the rest of your little lives!' he proclaimed.

One of the boys leaned over to a friend and commented, 'He'll be showing us again how his magic really has fooled him all along.'

Jargo finally got them to sit down and pay attention. He slipped his hand into his velvet pouch and whipped out the deck of cards as if it was candy. For a split second, all the children held their breaths. This put a smile on his face.

'Behold, kids. What looks a like an ordinary deck of cards is actually an ordinary deck of cards!'

'Allow me to demonstrate by first taking the cards out of the box,' he said, and slid them out like an ogre treading on a banana peel. His action lacked a bit of grace, sending cards flying all over the place. Without missing a beat, he added, 'This is a game we call fifty-two pick-up!'

Before he had a chance to show them the proper trick, he noticed out the corner of his eye that someone had moved in behind him. He felt a soft tap on his shoulder, and heard someone clearing his throat in his ear.

Jargo sat still for a moment and asked, 'Is there something with which I may help you?'

'In fact, there is,' came the response. 'The council requires you urgently in its meeting chambers, as something of great importance has risen!'

Within moments, the figure had vanished.

Not entirely sure whether to continue with the lesson, Jargo found himself a little disappointed. He was certain this time that the trick was going to work. Even if he was the only one who thought so, the thought still made him feel happy. But he sensed the urgency of the meeting, especially since he had never been formally invited to the council chambers before. Meetings in these chambers happened rarely, and when they did occur, it was often the case that some wizard would be buried the next day. On the upside, tea and rich fungus cake would be served. This was what most wizards looked forward to about council meetings.

He rose from the park bench and dismissed the boys. They took again to playing among the trees, racing pieces of wood down the brook, or conjuring up some rather bright rope for skipping games.

He turned and walked to the main entrance of the Palace, while running his fingers through the brush that ran alongside the cobbled walkways. He paused for a moment at the bottom of the stairs and looked up. A wand attached to a hand started to wave outside one of the windows that overlooked the Palace. Within moments, he felt his body being pulled into an incredibly small place and being plucked out from the other side by what felt like tweezers. Turning and looking around, he found six pairs of eyes, which looked as if they'd fallen into a pot of soup, staring back at him.

Grenger got up from his chair.

'Welcome Jargo. I hope you don't mind us hurrying you along.'

Checking to see if his head was still attached to his neck, Jargo replied, 'Well, as long as everything is still in its rightful place, I need not worry.'

'There's a seat over there if you want to sit down. In this case, I suggest you do.'

'Oh ... well ... maybe I will, then,' he said hesitantly.

Grenger cleared his throat and took a sip of fermented tea he had brewed up with a flick of his wand.

'Would you care for a cup?'

'I think I will pass this time, thank you.'

'I understand that you enjoy your time with the children,' he said, 'but I am sure that once we discuss what has come to our attention, you will understand our disruption.'

Jargo leaned into his chair and rubbed his nose.

'In the early hours of this morning, this arrived via Arrow Mail,' Grenger said, laying a brown parchment, tied up with a red silk ribbon, before Jargo.

Mezzar stretched over the heavy wooden table and intercepted the parchment. Not everyone was informed of issues outside the realm of the Palace. Most were not even informed if there had been a change in the weather.

Jargo held the parchment in his hands tightly and stared across the table. A slurp was heard from one of the council members.

'Pardon,' said Ceeder. 'Someone had to break the silence.'

'We are all waiting patiently for Jargo to read the note,' Grenger added. 'Let's not all jump at once to help him along.'

Jargo looked down at the red ribbon and twirled one end around his finger. He was not sure if what was going to be read was at all in his interests. He looked over towards Grenger, who was nodding impatiently.

He sat straight up in his chair and opened up the parchment carefully, almost expecting a spell to jump out and turn him into a frog.

'Dear High Council,' read Jargo slowly:

It is with great concern that we send this note. I trust that once you have read it, you will take action immediately. The Mother Queen requests all towns to send a worthy warrior to aid her with a quest of great importance! Please ensure that this warrior is sent before the next view of the three-quarter suns.

Yours faithfully,

King Sorbus.

'Oh, great,' Jargo said aloud.

'Great it is,' Grenger answered. 'King Sorbus did use the word *great* a lot, didn't he?'

'What does this have to do with me? Why was I asked to read it?'

'So many questions. I like a wizard with questions. Always searching for the truth.'

Jargo looked around the room, confusion all over his face.

'Is *anyone* here going to shed some light on the subject?'

He noticed Grenger smiling. With his arms behind his back, Grenger walked over to the window that overlooked the entire Palace, and took a deep breath.

'Do you smell that?' he asked.

'The silver onions they are making for lunch?' asked Ceeder.

'No, I don't mean *that*.'

He turned towards Jargo, pointing at him.

'Do *you* smell what I smell?'

'I am not sure what I should be smelling. The only thing I smell here is confusion!' he said, annoyed.

A bird chirped in the distance, then suddenly stopped as if someone had clamped a hand over its beak.

Grenger clapped his hands together eagerly and shouted, 'Opportunity! Opportunity is what I smell here!'

Opportunity was the last word going through Jargo's mind. The mere idea that there was an opportunity to seize left a knot in his stomach.

'Let me fill in the gaps for you,' continued Grenger.

'The council and I have discussed the matter thoroughly, and feel that we need to send our strongest wizard.'

'So, what does this have to do with me? Oh ... wait ... you think ... this wizard is *me*?' said Jargo, pointing at himself.

In the Palace of Elders was a hall of fame where wizards were honoured for their conquests around the kingdom. Marble statues crowded the hall. The figures stood tall above the sandy ground, watching over the rest of the Palace way below their feet. One of the retired wizards was taking his daily walk through the Hall of Fame when he noticed that one of the statues' heads was turned towards another. He frowned.

'That doesn't happen often. Come to think of it, that's *never* happened. News must have crept through the air foul enough to be able to do this to marble,' he thought. The wizard grabbed one of his hands with the other and felt for his pulse, making sure he was still alive. The dreamlike feeling of the moment left a cold, sunken feeling in what was left of his frail body.

'Yes, I suppose this kind of comment does turn heads,' said Grenger.

Jargo noticed that most of the council seemed to be looking the other way. Even Ceeder wasn't looking at his normal spot, the breakfast table.

'But why has the council decided that I have what it takes to be this wizard destined for glory?'

'The decision was based on several things – your age being one of them.'

'Somehow I think my age has very little to do with my ability to achieve whatever the Mother Queen desires.'

Grenger raised his forefinger to his lips for a moment. 'May I ask you this?'

'What?'

'Are you able to make the trip before the three moons set?'

Jargo hesitated for a moment. 'I suppose …'

'That settles it, then. Council, if you please, a quick vote. All in favour of Jargo going, say Aye.'

Jargo looked around the room in disbelief. As one, the council said Aye solemnly.

'Good,' said Grenger, the relief visible in his face.

'Now, who will join me for a cup of hot fermented orange tea and a fresh cinnamon moss cookie?'

Several murmurs of approval went around the room. The council members stood, then drifted towards the breakfast table.

Clothes flew around Jargo's room as he struggled to find what he was looking for. With much scepticism, and several scratches to the head later, he turned. Without looking, he walked straight into a closed door. He rubbed his forehead, enjoying the fact the pain took his mind off things for just a few moments. Then he beamed a satisfied smile.

'At last! I found it!' he announced, pushing his pointed hat straight.

He held up his most prized possession towards the light. It gleamed as the rays of sun bounced of its magnificent shape. It was the wand he truly admired, the only one that worked perfectly every time – like a two-headed coin in a toss-up tournament. He singled out a fine velvet pouch that seemed to change colour as you looked at it. He carefully examined the wand before he placed it into the pouch.

Jargo had only ever owned two wands. The first was the spiral wand, which he used for day-to-day things, mostly when he was too lazy to do them himself. Then there was the black wand. It was made of Shadow Wood, which only grew in the deepest part of the kingdom where very few wizards ever found themselves. The wood was so dark that even the sun's rays seemed to get lost in it. Some wizards said you could hear the rays ask the wood for directions to get out.

The black wand was only ever used when it was deemed necessary, as it had extreme power. Even the most experienced wizard had difficulty controlling it. During Jargo's illustrious career, he'd obtained the secrets of controlling the black wand. He had often wondered why he was given this priceless information, but now he understood. The black wand's secret was kept locked up in an ancient scroll, heavily guarded by bounty ogres, monstrous bodyguards specifically assigned to safeguard secrets. Very few were able to persuade an ogre to give up secrets they were ordered to protect, and only a handful could defeat one. Jargo was one of the élite to have this achievement behind his name, but he thought this success was a matter of luck. Either way, fortune favours the brave, as they say; a critical mind would have thought it favours the bold.

He gazed at the pouch for a moment, then tucked it into a hidden pocket inside his robe. Then, he made sure he had everything he needed for the trip ahead.

'Wand: check.'

'Black wand: check.'

'Hat on straight: check.'

'Pouch on side: check.'

'Bag of tricks: check.'

He stood, leaning on the window sill, then glanced up at the sky. Ensuring there was enough wind in the air, he took a deep breath, then exhaled.

'Right. The time has come, I suppose. Home, I bid you a decent goodbye and hope we meet up again soon.'

Jargo walked to the centre of the room and straightened his robe. He dusted it off carefully and focused on the wall in front of him. He circled his spiral wand three times, clockwise.

'Places I want to be!' he called, then vanished, leaving a puff of dust behind.

A mouse, hiding in the closet, coughed.

Then sneezed.

And wiped its nose.

Chapter 4

The Caves of Deelg

It was not often that one heard the sounds of water gushing down at the Caves of Deelg, where the powerful dragons lie and rest; rather, the silence that protected their world was a common sound. Dekrin couldn't seem to stop gulping water from the rivers that ran through the caves.

In between slurps of water, words burped out.

'My mouth is on fire!'

'Son, in case you hadn't noticed ... you are a dragon!' said Barzeg.

It was midday.

The Caves of Deelg lay carefully hidden in a lush, dark valley. The mist hung, lazy, through the forests; pathways wound between the caves. A mist not so dense that you could not take two steps without bouncing off another dragon, but the kind that made you blink twice, thinking your eyesight had gone for a loop. Or that you may have forgotten you were wearing a permanent eye-patch.

The sun never seemed to visit here much, as the tall mountains surrounding the valley never gave it chance to show its true warm personality. The tall shoulders of rocks seemed to touch every corner of the sky. These overgrown mountains seemed to stand at attention all the time, never having the chance to settle quietly behind the stars that illuminated the shades of grey within the mountains' aged, irregular grooves and overhanging cliffs.

'Son, how are you ever going to be a true dragon if you cannot breathe fire?'

'It feels like I have heartburn.'

'Well, that's a good sign!' smiled Barzeg.

'I prefer to fly around, if it's fine with you. Look – I could use my tail!'

Dekrin swung his tail around like it was a frustrated blacksmith's hammer trying to straighten a bent sword.

'Not bad, but I don't think it will help in long-range attacks.'

'But do all dragons have to be bad?'

'No, just us,' said Barzeg.

A sudden wind swept through the valley. It gathered up several scattered leaves, forming a whirlwind of dust and sand.

'I sense a storm coming through here any minute,' said Barzeg.

'Come on, Dekrin. Let us go home. I am sure there is still enough Flurt meat left to eat. You need all the energy for tomorrow's practice.'

Dekrin never liked his name much. In fact, Dekrin wanted to be a normal dragon. But he'd been born into a family infamous for being the most vicious and hated dragon kind. He enjoyed just being a dragon, without having to wreak havoc on some poor town. Dekrin tried to disown himself, and changed his name to something he felt was as normal as they come. He often flew over the faraway towns where humans lived happily, hoping he would pick up some name he could call his own.

One day, he flew over a human town and saw a child pointing at him in the sky. The child's mother came running out, screaming, 'Son, come inside immediately before that menace eats you for lunch!' But the child just stood in awe. His smile beamed brightly as Dekrin flew by. This made the young dragon very happy. It occurred to him that the child was not scared of him. Dekrin did not like the idea of being called a menace, though. But he did love the boy's name. So Dekrin decided to name himself after the beaming child, Denniz.

'You will not be known as Denniz!' shouted Barzeg.

Dekrin had to think fast.

'But Dad, while I was in flight circling the humans' village,' he said nervously, 'I overheard them shouting I was a menace. I didn't think Dekrin the Menace had a nice ring to it. So I am calling myself Denniz. It rhymes with menace too.'

Barzeg looked in disbelief and shook his head.

He walked around in circles for a while, then stopped.

'You know, son, I admire your spirit. Finally you are seeing the light in which we hold our family's name. Not so sure about the Denniz part, but the menace has a good sound to it.'

Dekrin smiled and flicked his tail through the air.

'Son, shall we begin today's lesson?'

"Father, I think all these lessons have been the same.' remarked Dekrin.

'This is because you still have not found it in yourself to breathe the fire of destruction!'

Dekrin paused.

'Could I not refer to it as the Recreational Fire? As in, use it only when you need it?'

Barzeg glared at his son with one eye and stomped his foot. This meant he was to be taken seriously.

Dekrin quickly straightened up and raised his voice.

'Let the lesson begin, to develop the Fire of Destruction!'

His father turned, shaking his head.

The dragons of Deelg were a dying breed. They were sought after, not for their power, but for their body parts. Among witches, wizards and potential potion makers, most parts of a dragon were considered more valuable than gold. Dragon parts could help develop potions to heal or destroy. Only a few dragons were brave enough to sacrifice some of their valuable assets for what they truly admired: gems. A combination of crushed gems and fire breath could produce an elixir that could give any creature eternal life. Only the dragons of Deelg knew how to make it. All other creatures tried to convince these dragons to give up their ultimate secret. Some dragons had lost their lives protecting it, while others fought against misfits who were dying for it to land in the wrong hands.

So far, the secret had been kept safe after all these millennia. And Barzeg intended it to stay so, but it would only be a matter of time before he became tired of fighting to protect it, or before the day came when he would be defeated. He wished his one and only son would learn the vital mechanics of keeping the secret alive and safe. If only Dekrin could learn to breathe fire.

'Now do you understand why we need you to develop this skill? It is, of course, to guarantee our existence for the future.'

'I think it is a lot of responsibility for a young dragon like myself,' replied Dekrin.

'Well, understand that you are the only one left, so you will have to live with the consequences.'

Dekrin muttered under his breath.

'Normal, normal is all I want.'

Barzeg pointed with his clawed tail to the spot where his son needed to stand.

'Now. Legs apart like we've done before. Lower your tail slightly, giving your body a chance to lean forwards. Arms slightly forward and raised. Yes, just like that. I must say, you do have this part down well.'

Dekrin looked at his father and asked, 'Then why am I not getting it right?'

'Son, it requires a lot more effort than being able to stand. You need to realise that this is just the start of it – there are many more lessons, in which you need to learn to breathe fire while in the air.'

Dekrin thought about it for a moment and smiled. He liked the idea of lighting up the evening skies and actually being able to see where he was flying through the hanging mist. All of a sudden, he wanted to be grown up and on his own. The thought of being in control like his father inspired him to get this lesson licked. And not blown like a candle in the wind.

Dekrin assumed the position and went through the steps in his head. Thinking out loud, he blurted, 'Legs out. Tail down. Lean forward. Arms out slightly. Head up. Breathe in. Let it burn within your throat. Do not be alarmed.'

He began to feel a sudden gush of air which warmed the insides of his chest. Could this be really what he, and especially his father, had waited for, for so long?

'BURP!'

Barzeg looked on in disbelief.

'Oops, sorry, Father. Too much rotten Flurt-meat build-up from last night. I told you we need a fresh batch. Although, I must admit I do feel much better. If I do enough of those in a row, some fire is bound to come out eventually?'

'Son, I think I need to go and find some fresh meat for tomorrow. You just keep practising. And make sure you practise your dive-bombs from the jade cliff over there.'

Dekrin was only too happy to practise his dive bombs, as a distraction from what he could not do. Barzeg flew off, leaving a whirl of dust around his son. Dekrin watched as his father disappeared into the shadows of the cliffs.

'Why do I bloody have to gallop this way? Why could it not be Ravells?' shouted Andrews.

The brown horse galloped through the overgrown forest and the leaves raised a trail behind. Archer Andrews was asked to deliver The Message to the Caves of Deelg, being the quickest around these dark areas – only because he was genuinely afraid of the dark and knew it was in his best interest to spend as little time here as possible. He knew if he was caught anywhere here near dusk, he would go off his rocker shortly afterwards. His mind played tricks on him when the night came out to play. And he felt it never played fair. It always felt as if something, or someone, was out to get him. The upside to his paranoia was that he became one of the best shots in the kingdom. His strategy was simply to carry too many arrows with him, so he could shoot at just about anything that crossed his path. His accuracy had kept him out of plenty of hot water in the past.

He had almost reached the mail post, and knew that all it would take was a quick aim and an even quicker turn of his horse to be done and out of there. He approached the clearing, zoned in on the mail post and smiled slightly. He raised his bow and took out the arrow-covered letter. He fired at his target. As the arrow left his bow, he noticed something in the corner of his eye. It seemed to be a rather large dragon, dive-bombing towards him from a green cliff.

Andrews turned white as snow.

'Oh my,' he said, trembling.

'I am going to die! Let's get out of here, Horse!'

He grabbed the reins and jerked the horse's head in the opposite direction.

Dekrin started his descent from the cliff like he always did – with his eyes closed, and roaring with delight. To any other type of creature, this roar sounded as menacing as ever. To him, it was the sound of pure enjoyment.

He opened up one eye to gauge how far he was from the ground, when he noticed a cloud of dust and leaves and heard a human voice.

'AAAAAAAAHHHHHH!'

'NOT GOING TO DIE TODAY!'

Dekrin barely made out that it was a human on a horse before the pair disappeared into the overgrown forest.

He wondered what that had been all about. As he flew back up, he heard a distant ringing of a bell. He recognised it as the mail bell. Not sure how long ago it had last rang, he was only too eager to see if any mail awaited him. His wings flapped loudly as he sought some speed. Within seconds, he had reached the clearing. He landed carefully, not wanting to knock anything over with his wings. The mail target was still swinging slightly, and something gleamed. He walked over to look. It was definitely an arrow, and a letter with golden thread had been tied to it. The letter swayed gently in the breeze.

Dekrin took the arrow like a toothpick between two claws and extracted it carefully. The golden thread gleamed. He smiled. He had a feeling this could be very important, and knew he had to get it to his father urgently.

He took flight into the blue skies, leaving the mail post to sway some more in his wake.

The cave was dimly lit. The few fires that burned within it give it an eerie glow. Deep inside, Barzeg was hard at work. He limped over to his gem stash and took out a few red and blue ones. One side of the cave was neatly carved out into a pestle. The mortar was Barzeg's thumping fist. He laid the gems into the pestle and started to bash them into pieces. Every so often, he would breathe some fire onto them. The heat made the gems brittle, which made the crushing so much easier. A dragon's breath was hundred times hotter than any fire a human could make. The chemicals in the soul and body of a dragon were sacred, accessible to no other creatures. Only a dragon's breath could make gems brittle. The more oxygen a dragon could inhale, the more powerful and dangerous the fire-blast it breathed would be. The bigger the dragon, the more devastating the flame.

Concentration lined Barzeg's scaly face as he turned the hard gems into nothing but liquid. A cup-shaped rock stood nearby. He grabbed it and drained some of the gem liquid from the pestle into the cup. Dekrin swooped into the cave, his face alight. He was eager to know whether the message had any bearing on the dragons of Deelg.

'Father! This just came,' he said breathlessly.

'What did, Son?'

'This!' He pointed to the message with his tail.

Barzeg looked up from the cup to the scroll. Dekrin walked over quickly and laid the scroll down in front of Barzeg, who seemed interested in the message for a moment.

'Son, I notice this scroll has come from the king and queen directly.'

'Oh, it has? Oh wow, then it must be important?'

'Importance is as only as good as parchment it is written on. Please dispose of it immediately.'

Dekrin frowned and moved closer to the scroll.

'But Father, I do not understand. If it's important, is it not worth a read to see what the kingdom requires from us?'

Barzeg turned and stomped around the cave. He did not like to associate himself with any type of creature in the kingdom, least of all humans.

'Son, I will explain only once. We DO NOT associate ourselves with any race. I cannot recall when last the kingdom helped out the dragons of Deelg when we needed them in desperate times. There was a time where we were being exploited for their medicines. A high price was put on any dragon's head. Creatures came in their droves to kill every one of us, purely to get rich. Some failed, while others succeeded. The creatures at times even put their differences behind them and teamed up to destroy us. Most of our tribe had to flee to a different sector of the kingdom, only reachable by a long-distance flight.'

Dekrin leaned back against the cave wall, listening intently.

'Luckily, we managed to find a treacherous mountain range, which could only be found through flight. Luckily, too, we were the only ones at the time who could fly. Our ancestors carved these caves deep into the mountains so we could live in peace and protect our secret.'

Dekrin looked at his father, silent, thinking.

Barzeg continued.

'You must be wondering why there are so few of us left. Our isolation over the millennia made us lose contact with our allies. Our stores of gems started to diminish. It caused many of our great warriors to age and, in time, to die out.'

Dekrin looked out towards the cave mouth. Is this all I can aspire to? he asked himself. This was not a world in which he wanted to live. He wanted a world where he could fly free without prejudice, where he would be respected as one of the races, admired, but never feared. His shoulders sank as he realised this would never be.

'Son, you understand why we cannot make contact with the outside world anymore. My father left us many years ago, and promised me that one day it would be different. I have tried many times to change the future for us, but it seems the chance is getting smaller with time.'

Barzeg grabbed the unopened scroll and handed it back to Dekrin. He took it slowly from his father's hand.

'Please, son, for the sake of our existence – please go outside and destroy this. Maybe this is your chance to breathe real life into a future without hope by destroying this with your fiery blast.'

The light from outside pulled Dekrin closer. Barzeg limped as he turned and carried on working on the potion.

'Father, why are you limping?' Dekrin asked as he looked back at Barzeg.

'Well, I think I got tangled up in one of the forest trees as I was hunting for Flurt meat again. You do know how tricky they can be between the trees,' he said hesitantly.

'Yes, I know.'

Dekrin turned and stepped out of the cave. The afternoon sun caught his saddened face. He took to the skies and flew to his favourite jade cliff. The mountains made everything below seem so insignificant. He felt that he was meant for greater things. The golden thread around the scroll glittered. He looked down at it.

Curiosity never got the better of him, but today was an exception. He felt this message had to reach someone. Why else would the kingdom send it as far as the Caves of Deelg? He thought about going against all his father stood for, but worried that his father might not be alive for much longer. Dekrin looked all around him to make sure no one was watching. He ran one of his sharp claws over the golden thread. It dropped to the ground like sand through an hourglass. The scroll unrolled.

Dear High Council. It is with great concern that this note reaches you.

He wondered and smiled at the word 'great'. He knew this was meant to fall into his father's hands. But he knew, too, that this would certainly be his one chance to prove not only to his father, but to all the living races out there, that the dragons of Deelg were to be respected.

It was time to make a decision. A decision to hurry to the kingdom as fast as he could. Barzeg would be busy for days perfecting the potion. He had time to disappear, to make a difference. He stood tall and let out a huge roar, like a fire-blast dying to come out. But he knew that now was not the right time to practise. He had a kingdom to save!

Chapter 5

Aldedde

Telling a troll 'Any slower and you'll be walking backwards' would, more often than not, get you killed.

Or, at the very least, trodden on.

Severely.

Trolls. Immensely overgrown beings who seemed to take up a lot of space. But they never seemed to think so. Then again, trolls never seemed to think.

The saying around this part of the woods was 'There is bound to be a sharp blade in a pile of very blunt ones.'

This, of course, applied to trolls, if you had at least a week to dig really deeply.

A troll village had, in no hurry, developed between Silvercrown and the Caves of Deelg. This village, called Aldedde, unintentionally occupied space. This space was in turn, occupied by trolls. Trolls, on any given day, disliked doing much. Their day consisted mostly of eating and preparing food to be eaten. Their oversized bodies needed loads of energy to get through the day.

It was early morning and fires were heard crackling through the murmuring of trolls trying to maintain conversation. These conversations often included tremendous amounts of grunting and mumbling, and tremendous amounts of silence. They weren't ones for deep thoughts, but they managed to get their point across anyway.

There was one troll who took special interest in day-to-day things. Clannk was a hulk of enthusiasm. He enjoyed food so much that he decided to become the local cook and baker just so he could have his cake and eat it. He enjoyed anything edible that he could get his bulky hands on. He especially enjoyed having enough ingredients to make up some of his own dishes. Clannk discovered an unbelievable pie-filling recipe, for example. It was his speciality. He aptly called it hollow pie.

Clannk waved through his window with his oversized hand. The window looked onto a stone-faced home, occupied by the only female troll in the village. Yulo was a little smaller than the rest of the trolls but she did not seem to mind. Her face was slightly more feminine than the males', in that she did not have stubble as a beard, but as hair on her head. Pieces of mattered hair seemed to bounce off the sides of her head. They'd been tied into two pigtails. Her smaller size allowed her to walk with less drag in her stride. Trolls appeared top-heavy, and their feet dragged, one in front of the other, as they walked.

Not many females were able to contend with these oversized squares. But Yulo managed to maintain some normality within the camp. She waved back as she looked out of her window, which was always open – troll dwellings were made out of huge rectangular blocks of stone piled on top of each other and, with trolls not being great architects, the gaps between the stones made plenty of windows.

'Nice morning?' asked Clannk.

'Suppose,' replied Yulo. 'Wot you doin'?'

'Same. Like yesterday,' said Clannk.

'Want to drink musky brew? Eat hollow pie?' asked Clannk.

'Okay.'

'See you.'

Trolls never beat around the bush – unless they are using the bush to beat somebody up. They were not normally violent beings, but if they could not convey their message through words, they resorted to conveying it physically. Most often, the one who could communicate better came off second best.

Clannk stood at his pantry and scratched through the half-full jars. He clinked his way through a few before he managed to find one with a handwritten label partially attached to it. It read *Brind S-N-A-P-S*.

'Good!' he grunted.

He unscrewed the lid and took a pinch of the jar's contents out with his colossal fingers. It seemed his pinch could cover a human from head to toe, but looked to be the right amount for the pie. He leaned over the stone table and grabbed a wooden spoon that looked more like a tree with a dent in it. Grabbing some flour and water and pouring it into a bowl, he started stirring the mixture clockwise. Making sure he was concentrating hard, he counted loudly.

'Ughhh.'

'One.'

'Um.'

'Two.'

'Ughhh.'

'One …'

Flour puffed everywhere. Amazingly, dough started to form inside the bowl.

On the outskirts of Aldedde ran a stream that carved a way through the forests. Trolls loved to sit near it, under the overgrown trees, and to soak up as much sun as possible. It gave them an excuse to recharge whichever batteries kept them running. 'Refuel the mule' was often muttered among those who dared discuss trolls' intelligence. Not that trolls seemed to mind the comments being made about them – they simply didn't understand the comments, so their feelings were never hurt. The only feeling trolls had was hunger. Often it would take a troll a whole day to prepare a meal, only for the meal to be eaten within minutes, and for the discussion to move immediately to what the next course would be.

Blangg leant against a coarse-barked tree. The oversized troll's pants were tied to his waist with a rope, their torn legs hugging his awkwardly shaped carves. He was scratching his nose. A troll's nose was always a discussion point among other beings in the kingdom – they were noses that were impossible to miss. It was said that the first part of a troll to turn a corner was its nose. Some said the nose hairs turned the corner first; either way, the first thing you noticed about a troll was related to the breathing apparatus of these bulky characters. Not too much gossip surrounded trolls, however, as trolls never seemed to be too bothered about it.

Blangg noticed that something had appeared on his crooked finger. He examined it with intent. The oddly shaped object he could not identify. He decided to shoot it off his finger with his thumb. The unwanted blob flew through the air, like a stone shot from under a chariot crossing a rocky service road. It flung itself right across the grassed area where he sat, lodging itself halfway up a tree.

Something was irritating him. He sat up for a moment to ponder what it could be. A feeling had been poking his empty mind, on which he couldn't quite put his finger.

Blangg reluctantly got up, and stretched.

Bright sun rays followed Archer Andrews. As good a shot as he was, he never had the time to think twice about where he aimed his arrows. The pressure to send Arrow Mails urgently made Archer Andrews anxious. He didn't like the look of the messages sealed with a golden thread. It meant that something or someone in the kingdom was in trouble. And he did not like this one bit. But a job had to be done. So he rode his best white horse along the roads throughout the kingdom. He galloped as fast as his beautiful white stallion could muster. Andrews leant into the horse's neck as hard as he could, to get as much out of him as possible. He knew how to ride a horse to its maximum. He knew how to shoot from one too. And today was no exception. For some reason, the kingdom always seemed to 'forget' to send Arrow Mail to Aldedde. The kingdom felt that its messages wouldn't cross the trolls' minds with any meaning. But the kingdom was in dire straits, so the message needed to cross all avenues of the living world.

Archer Andrews took a corner in the forest with dust rising into the air to mark his presence. He bent from side to side as he rode his stallion hard. The horse snorted with every stride, yet enjoyed galloping at its fastest pace. Andrews knew he had only one shot around the last corner and ensured himself it would be his best. He reached for his bow and pulled it out in front of him. His left arm reached to the back of him, grabbing an Arrow Mail. He inserted it to the bow and pulled back at the string. The bow pulled tight within his grasp. He closed his left eye. His right eye opened wide and sought out the target, which hung motionless, unused for a very a long time. The time had come to wake up the post, Andrews thought. He breathed in and released his left hand. The Arrow Mail arced its way towards the target, pierced the post, and shattered it into tiny pieces. The shards flew up into the air like the splashes of a stone hitting water.

Although Archer Andrew had already left the clearing, the Arrow Mail kept on flying through the air. It was determined to embed itself in something. There was an object in its path. The arrow flew right into it.

PTTTWWANNNGGGHHH!

The forest opened towards Aldedde. A path wound its way towards the village. Blangg had meandered through the forest and found the path. As he walked, he heard a creaking sound; every time he stopped to look behind him, it stopped.

Clannk heard a knock on his wall. He turned to look, and saw Yulo coming in.

'Just in time,' he said.

'Good, I am starving.'

He pointed to what resembled a chair made out of stone. A bigger rock lay next to it, giving the impression there was a table to sit at. A few more stones lay around the house, trying to do their best to fulfil some purpose.

A rich, sweet smell wafted through the household.

'Musky brew?' he offered.

'To the top please,' said Yulo, pointing out to the wooden cup in front of her.

Clannk smiled as he filled two cups on the stone table. He turned towards the window and grabbed a huge crusted pie from the sill. It was golden brown, its five holes oozing flavours. The pie certainly looked good; it would be eaten in no time.

He cut the pie into four really big pieces and offered one of them to Yulo. She immediately raised her hands to grab the biggest piece. Both of them sat down and munched on the freshly baked hollow pie.

Hollow pie had always been Clannk's favourite invention. Its ingredients were always readily available, and the pie was very simple to make. It had sweet and savoury flavours, consisting of a few fruits and dried meat that Clannk would wrap in tree-leaves and ferment for a few days. There was, however, a secret ingredient – and Clannk was the only one who knew how much of it to put in. It was named hollow pie for a reason; when you had a slice, it felt like you had not eaten anything. It left a hollow in your stomach. It tasted so good that you kept on eating, until there was nothing left.

Yulo swallowed her last piece of pie and washed it down with a big gulp of musky brew. She turned and burped across the table.

'Thanks for the compliment,' Clannk replied with a smile.

'Do you have plans for today?'

Yulo scratched her temple and wiped the crumbs off her mouth.

'I need to go and count the animals. Something strange has been going on. Some went missing.'

'Missing?' Clannk frowned.

'Missing.'

'How do the animals go missing?'

Yulo got up from the hard seat and strolled to the door.

'This is what I need to go and look for,' she replied.

For a split second this bothered Clannk. But his mind was instantly preoccupied with his next meal. Yulo turned and waved goodbye as she left his home.

The sun stood high above every scattered cloud in the morning sky. The day baked every home in Aldedde, forcing every dweller to seek some sort of shade outside. Some leant against trees, while others lay in long patches of tall grass chewing on the end of a sprout.

A shuffle of feet was heard down the path that left the village – a shuffle, and a creaking sound. Blangg entered the village, looking puzzled. Through his window, Clannk noticed that Blanng looked a little out of sorts. Blanng always looked out of shorts too, his shorts hanging low, barely held up by a dusty old piece of rope.

Clannk walked out to greet Blanng.

'Morning, Blanng. What's up?'

'Morning. Not sure, but I think something is following me.'

'Any reason why?' asked Clannk.

'Well it started when I was lying in the field, having a snooze. A noise woke me,' he explained with his hands in the air.

'Then when I got up I felt throbbing from the back of my head. I thought it was from the noise. I turned around to look what woke me.'

Clannk stepped aside as Blanng demonstrated in detail how he got up and rubbed his head and then turned around.

Clannk noticed something peculiar on the back of Blanng's head. It looked like an arrow had lodged into it.

'Um, Blanng, do you know you have something sticking out of your head?'

Blanng turned around and tried to see if he could notice anything. He kept on turning in circles, so many times that he spun out of control and hit the ground with another loud thud.

Clannk held out his hand to pull Blanng back up onto his feet. He looked at the arrow, and yanked it out with one pull.

'Ouch!' moaned Blanng.

Clannk laughed.

'Lucky it was not a whole long way in.'

He noticed there was some sort of paper stuck on the arrow. The paper was torn; it barely hung from a piece of string. Clannk tried to unravel it, but it tore in his bulky hands. The paper had a few scribbles on it. He could make out a few words, but not the letter's meaning. He recognised the king and queen's mark. The only way for him to understand the letter would be to make a trip up to the castle and ask the royalty for some clarity.

'Thanks, Clannk. Head doesn't hurt anymore!' said Blanng enthusiastically.

Clannk patted Blanng on the back and walked off. He knew he needed to get going; it took half a day to get to the castle. Already, the walls of his home shone in the heat. He figured that if he needed to stop and eat something on the long trip ahead, it had better be worth eating. He went to his pantry and plucked a few ingredients from a few jars. He stuffed them it into a well-used, dark leather pouch, tied the pouch closed with some coarse string, and shoved the bag into his worn pants. A head popped into his house.

Yulo looked puzzled.

'You going somewhere?' she asked.

Clannk walked up to her and put his arm on her shoulder.

'I have to take this to the kingdom. Don't know what it says, but need to find out if it is meant for our village.'

He showed Yulo what was left of the letter. Yulo looked at it for a bit and handed it back to him.

'I guess you are the only one who seems to bother with things around here.'

'I suppose,' he replied.

She hugged him briefly, then made way for him as he walked past.

Sir Lankshire trotted slowly through the woods on his white stallion. A couple of soldiers on horseback followed carefully behind. They were patrolling the forests on the king's orders.

Lankshire muttered to himself. One of the patrolmen heard a flutter of words.

'What is it that you mumbled, Sir?' he questioned.

'For your information, I DO NOT MUMBLE,' said Lankshire sternly.

'What I said was, I am not sure why we were given this job to patrol the boundaries of the castle.'

One of the patrolmen put his hand up in the air.

'What is it, Patrolman Two?' Lankshire said, agitated.

The patrolman looked around, then said, 'Is it not perhaps because we were not qualified for the quest?'

Lankshire turned and raised his eyebrows.

'Qualified? QUALIFIED?' Of course we are qualified. Willing we are NOT.'

He stopped his stallion and turned to his men.

'If there is one certain thing, it is that we protect the kingdom at all costs. What would happen if we chose to go on this quest? Who would protect the castle boundaries then?' he asked.

Patrolman One nodded in agreement.

'Ah, Sir. Spot on. You hit it right on the nose,' he said, tapping his own.

'Good thinking, Sir,' said Patrolman Two, winking at Patrolman One.

'Now, I suggest we go to off in that direction.' Lankshire pointed with his sword towards the east.

The patrols had always followed the rising and setting of the sun. This ensured that they covered all corners of the kingdom, and still made it back in time for the evening meal. During the evenings, the patrolmen congregated around a huge open fire, watching one of the kingdom's chefs struggle to cook a huge piece of meat stuck on a long piece of metal. Some of the knights enjoyed winding down the evening by swapping stories and drinking brew. Sir Lankshire was always the one to tell stories that were bigger than they really were. But it kept the other knights amused; they enjoyed setting off to bed with a smile on their faces.

Patrolman One looked after Sir Lankshire's left side. Patrolman Two, of course, protected his right. They knew their job was to protect the most knighted soldier in the kingdom. What they did not know that he was the only one knighted out of all the soldiers. And for good reason: none of them were really worth being knighted. Sir Lankshire had stumbled into the castle one day to regale the King with one of his exaggerated stories. King Sorbus was practising his sword bowing when Lankshire made an entrance. When King Sorbus did this, he always closed his eyes to ensure he appreciated who knelt in front of him. Lankshire had got his foot stuck in a fold of the carpet, and fallen face-first. He'd slid right under the king's nose. When the king's insignia sword touched anyone's shoulder as the king bowed, decorum stated that the person would indeed be knighted. King Sorbus wanted to avoid embarrassment, and promptly announced the knighthood bestowed on Lankshire, who became Sir Lankshire thereafter.

'Patrolmen, I see the sun is setting between those huge Rotting trees. It is getting late. Let us commence our final patrol in the last quadrant before we set off to seal the kingdom gates.'

Patrolman One scratched his ear with a twig.

'Which way is north again?' he asked innocently.

Sir Lankshire turned around in disgust.

'One, have I not taught you anything in the many years you have ridden next to me?'

'Sir, if I understand which way is north, I could work out which way is east. Always right ain't it?'

Patrolman Two tapped his nose twice and smiled.

'It is much easier if you know where west is and look the opposite way.' said Lankshire.

'Then what would I be looking at?' frowned One.

'Then you bloody would be looking at east, Patrolman!'

Patrolman One scratched his ear again and broke the twig in half.

Sir Lankshire noticed and leaned into One's face.

'Careful, that twig might just get lost in there,' he snarled.

Patrolman Two heard snapping branches up ahead. A few trees creaked as something tried to push them aside.

The three turned their horses, drew their swords and rode towards the noise.

Clannk kept to the path that led out of the Enslanted Forests of Rottingwood. He knew that if he kept to the well-worn walkways, he was sure to find his way to the castle gates. He was determined to find out what the torn parchment meant. He never fully understood why the kingdom involved them in anything over the years.

Everybody thought that the trolls of Aldedde could not think for themselves.

Clannk kept pushing the branches out of his way with his brute strength. He had barely made it to the clearing when he heard humans shouting and galloping hooves. He turned his head towards the dust cloud and saw three humans on horseback. He stopped and stared.

'Quickly, Patrolmen. Before THAT ... gets away!'

'Yes, Sir!' shouted both men.

'Forward ho!' Lankshire shouted.

'Time to shine for us all. Now here is a real story to tell tonight.'

Sir Lankshire knew his day would come; the day on which the laughter would settle down and some would admire his story. Today could be that day.

His sword gleamed in the late-afternoon sun, held high above his head as he rode. As they got closer to the Clannk, he shouted for the troll to stand still.

'Being! I command you to stop in your tracks!'

The white stallion quickly noticed it was indeed a troll and stopped in its own tracks. The knight flew over the horse's head, onto the ground. He landed and rolled onto his knees. In one hand, he held the silver sword, which he pointed at Clannk.

'Stop, Being!'

'Um, Troll.'

'Troll?' asked Lankshire, confused.

'Yup,' said Clannk.

'I have something ...' Clannk pointed at the parchment.

Both Patrolmen raised their swords and shouted.

'Halt! Very slowly. Now, one hand at a time.'

Sir Lankshire stood up and dusted himself off.

'Which hand first?' questioned Clannk.

'Um, north,' said Patrolman One.

Clannk froze, frowning.

Sir Lankshire scratched his head and raised his helmet slightly.

'Troll. Please excuse these nincompoops.'

'Clannk'

'Clank? What went clank?' the knight asked.

'Name's Clannk,' Clannk replied, with a slight smile.

'Troll Clannk, I am Sir Lankshire. And these are my patrolmen. Why do you find yourself in these protected parts of the woods?'

'This,' he replied, opening his bulky hand and pointing to what was left of the parchment.

All three of them leaned carefully and looked inquisitively into his hand.

'May I?' asked Lankshire.

'Yup,' replied Clannk.

He took the torn parchment out of the troll's hand and examined it. The setting sun caught it warmly.

'You ... had better come with us,' said Lankshire, as he climbed back onto his horse.

'There is someone who needs to see you urgently. Please follow us. I will ride out in front and One and Two will bring up the rear. So you will not get lost.'

'Follow? Where?' asked Clannk.

'To the castle, of course. Someone has been expecting you. He will be most pleased,' Lankshire smiled.

The horses broke into a trot; Clannk lumbered on between them. He looked at the sky and the setting sun. This made him hungry.

'Mmm,' he thought, then blurted, 'Hollow pie.'

Dribble ran from his mouth.

Chapter 6

The Kingdom

King Sorbus surveyed his feet as they placed themselves one in front of the other. They seemed to know where they were going, but the rest of his body didn't want to follow.

'Would you please stop pacing like that?' said the queen mother impatiently.

'It is making my nerves do the same, and I prefer for them to remain where they belong, which is in my body.'

His eyes never left the direction in which his feet were taking him, but Sorbus managed a nod to acknowledge the comment.

Mother Queen shuffled over to the window that covered most of one side of the lengthy room. She put her hands on the clay sill and sighed. Sorbus briefly glanced up and somehow got his brown leather slip-on shoes to walk in her direction. He paused next to her, placing his hand on her shoulder.

'They should be here soon. Of course, if the carriers ever got out there alive.'

'And more importantly, in one piece,' said Mother Queen.

'Piece or no piece, they will be here. I have a good feeling about it, Mother Queen.'

A Wallow-shriek Bird flew overhead, cursing as it landed on a nearby tree. The wind had picked up unrepentantly; it blew the bird right into an overhanging branch. The trees swayed rhythmically and the leaves shook.

Mother Queen's gaze picked up a commotion at the castle gates. Some men and a knight on horseback were trying their best to break through the bulky wooden doors. Over the wind came shouts from afar: 'Let us in, let us in!' A very senior guard holding a very tall spear rushed to the gate. He was senior not in experience but in age, with a stubbly grey beard covering his elastic cheeks. Several lines on his forehead created a permanent frown on his withered face.

'Who goes there?'

'It's bloody well us, Cedric!'

'Bloody well *who*?' asked Cedric.

'I have no time to play this game!' Sir Lankshire said, frustrated.

Cedric lowered his overgrown silver spear and pointed it towards the gate. He stood motionless and said, 'I have weapons, you know.'

'What? You and that oversized fork you call a spear?' snorted Lankshire.

Cedric tapped the gate with his spear. It made a slight thud against the wood.

'Let me say it can pierce right through this gate if I wanted it to.'

'Oh yes. And I can blow down this gate with one sneeze!'

Lankshire sat back on his silvery white stallion and laughed out loud. He pulled hard at the reins, making the horse neigh uncomfortably. He turned his stallion around and trotted away from the oversized tree which resembled some form of a gate.

'Hello?' whispered Cedric. His legs started to quiver in his dusty boots.

Silence fell; then came the sound of galloping hooves.

Cedric stood in fear and shouted.

'Hello? Is anyone there?'

Lankshire shouted towards the gate. 'Cedric, I suggest you open the gate. We have a rather worthy guest willing to fight for the queen's cause!'

Cedric scratched his forehead and looked behind him. He was not sure whether to believe Lankshire, but it did sound as if he was serious enough.

'Otherwise, he might just open up the gate himself.'

A huge thud was heard against the hulking castle gate. Cedric dropped his spear and ran over to the lever that lowered the gate.

'Please stand clear!' he shouted quickly.

There was a shuffling of horses, and with a stern voice, Cedric shouted.

'Releasing the gate!'

He pulled the lever with all his might as the chains holding the gate up ran through their wooden slots. The gate came crashing down, puffing up a cloud of dust and leaves.

Lankshire sat high upon his stallion and smiled.

'Thank you, Cedric. You may step aside to allow our guest in.'

Cedric looked up. Out of nowhere appeared the immensity of a troll.

'Duh, hello,' greeted Clannk.

Clannk looked lazily towards the castle and admired it for a while. He had never been to a castle and always wondered if he'd be able to walk within one's walls. Clannk was happy to know how easily he was able to walk freely around the castle. It was huge in comparison to where he had been living all his life.

'What is that?' Clannk said pointing.

A statue stood proudly in the centre of the castle's court. It was surrounded by lovely sculpted hedges and flowing stretches of beautifully green cut lawns. Clannk never imagined that nature could look so defined. He was happy to be able to see the beauty in it. Everything seemed to be in its rightful place, unlike his village, where the rest of the trolls liked to find things and put them in a place just because they could. Trolls never seemed to need a reason to do anything. Besides, nobody questioned their decisions. Those who thought about doing so did little more than think about it.

Quietly, of course.

To themselves.

Sir Lankshire jumped down from his horse and took off his studded helmet.

'This statue represents the protectors of the kingdom we live in.'

Clannk frowned. The lines on his forehead resembled canyons edged out through a rocky mountain.

'Them, the people who need help?'

Lankshire nodded in affirmation. He smiled and pointed up towards a cascade of stone stairs that led to a very small door. Clannk looked up towards the stairs, then looked back at all the knights staring at him.

'Up there, I go?'

Lankshire smiled and nodded.

He stomped past the statue, causing ripples in the nearby pond.

Cedric wiped his eyes and his brow with his sleeve,

then put his helmet back onto his head. He walked back over towards the open gate and stared across the silence of the forest. It seemed too quiet for a few moments, but the wind whistled through the trees to give the air a bit of relief from holding its breath. The leaves jingled eagerly as each tree tried to compete with its neighbour. He leaned over and grabbed the chain that hung lazily over the cog, giving it a decent pull. The chain tightened and a click was heard. With another pull to a different lever, the husky gate moved slowly back up and thudded to a close.

King Sorbus turned to Mother Queen and smiled.

'See, my dear. They are coming to your aid.'

She stood silently, staring out of the window.

'I am sure there will be more on its way. I imagine we will have many brave beings attempting to rescue the kingdom from evil.'

Mother Queen turned around and glared at King Sorbus. If glares could incinerate everything in their path, King Sorbus would look like burnt toast.

'Evil?' she questioned loudly.

'EVIL?'

'Evil did not do this. Evil would be far too careful to try to take over the kingdom again. I am certain IT paid the price the last time.'

'True. True,' said King Sorbus.

'But whom or what would want to do such a thing to the kingdom?'

'If I knew I wouldn't be here sitting and riding the kingdom's hopes on a HERO!'

King Sorbus quickly looked down and watched his feet shuffle.

The enormous window to the left of the sitting room could fit just about anything through itself. If the castle was just a little smaller, it could throw its very self out of that window. The queen mother pointed through it.

'And *that*?'

King Sorbus hurried to the window and looked up towards the sky. Something huge was flying in the distance.

'Is that what I think it is?'

King Sorbus blinked several times and looked. He was hoping he was not seeing what he saw.

'What are dragons doing in this part of the kingdom? Were they not banished from here after the tirade of the fire goblins?' she asked.

'They were, but you did say we should spread the word to all the villages across the kingdom.'

'I suppose. But did you really think they would send someone, or something, to come to the kingdom's aid?' she wondered, watching the troll make his way up the steps.

'Well, we don't bother trolls ... They leave us alone and we leave them alone. Much like the dragons of Deelg, we definitely leave them be,' she continued.

'I am just as confused as you are, Mother Queen.' Sorbus replied. 'I was truly hoping we would receive someone worthy from the cities and towns and villages who could actually save this kingdom. But let's not give up hope. We'll see what these creatures have to say for themselves.'

Dekrin swooped as he approached the castle. He flew through the air in spirals, and noticed the enormous window. It was arched and had a stone sill that protruded from the wall. Dekrin pulled out of his dive, slowly extending his leathery wings. They caught the air's resistance and slowed him down instantly. He extended his feet towards the window sill and pulled back with his wings to slow himself down for a soft landing. He took hold of the window sill firmly with his clawed feet, then quickly tucked in his wings to balance himself.

But a foot soon lost its grasp on the stony sill. It plucked out a large stone, sending it hurtling towards the ground. It narrowly missed one of the groundsmen who was shearing a bush. The groundsman looked up at the dragon in fear.

King Sorbus and Mother Queen stared at the dragon with their mouths open.

'I will, um, fix that.' Dekrin said apologetically.

She pointed at him, walking slowly towards him. King Sorbus extended his hand to stop her in her tracks.

'Dragon. Please get off there. I doubt our castle was meant to carry your weight and besides, that is no place for a dragon to sit!'

Dekrin looked around the huge balcony floor for a place to sit.

'So, King, where am I allowed to sit?'

'It's King Sorbus, Dragon. And you may sit over there.' He pointed to the floor below the window. Dekrin turned to his allotted corner, knocking over what looked like a very expensive and old vase. He froze on the spot at the sound of shattering porcelain.

'Just stand in the corner like a good dragon,' King Sorbus cautioned.

The dragon moved slowly into the corner, sat down, and tucked its tail in as far as it could go.

There were many steps to climb to the balcony, which was enclosed with a tiled roof and had many openings that resembled windows. Clannk made slow progress, eventually reaching his destination.

'Hello. I am Clannk.' He said to the king and queen, who stared at him as he entered.

'Greetings, Clannk. I am the queen and to my left is

King Sorbus. We run the kingdom. What brings you here?' she asked.

'This.'

Clannk opened his hand and looked at the torn parchment in his palm.

King Sorbus walked over and took it from him.

'Oh, yes. This. This – well what is left of it – was the golden-threaded letter we sent out to the kingdom's cities and villages. We have a situation.'

BANG!

Out of nowhere, a wizard suddenly appeared. As the dust settled around him, he took off his hat and wiped it briefly. Jargo put his hat back on and smiled at the king and queen.

'Good day to you, my king. I came as quickly as I could.'

'Greetings, Jargo. But why are you here? Are you not in retirement?'

'Well, technically I am. But for now, I am not. The Council of Elders thought I would be the perfect one to assist with your concerns.'

King Sorbus looked at Jargo for a brief moment.

'You mean you were voted to come here?'

'Well, yes, that too.'

He turned and looked around the room, noticing a dragon sitting very still in the corner, examining everyone with intent. To his left stood a rather oversized troll.

'Well, thank you for coming on such short notice. We do appreciate it,' the queen replied. A long wooden table stood across the middle of the balcony room. On either side sat enough chairs to surround the whole table. King Sorbus grabbed the end chair and pulled it out from under the table. He sat down.

'Everyone, take a seat while we wait for the others to arrive.'

Goblin City was hidden far away ...

'Take them out, carefully. And dispose of them,' grumbled Glasshook.

The four minions sang in unison.

'Don't worry, Master. For gold and greed.'

Glasshook pointed them out of the room with his hook.

Goblin City hid darkly on the outskirts of the kingdom. Every village, town and city was allowed to exist within the kingdom. Everyone and everything served a purpose. It allowed the kingdom to be in constant balance. Without calm and chaos the kingdom would cease to exist. However, the kingdom preferred if everything was calmer rather than chaotic. But chaos decided that it was its turn to awake from its lonely slumber.

Goblin City was run by the fire goblins, who were led by the feisty Glasshook. He was larger than all the other goblins. It was said he was an abomination to the Clan. However, he used his oversized body to his advantage; through the years, he took on the fire goblins' previous leaders. Glasshook won all his fights and claimed the highest rank. The other goblins were too afraid of his loyal army, who did most of his work for him. His soldiers were only too happy to do this, as the rewards were often great. Goblins loved gold and jewels as much as dragons did. Dragons shared a common interest and kept the goblins closer to their side than other beings would. The fire goblins were considered malicious and evil.

They always looked after their own interests. And greed was one of them.

The afternoon skies were warming up the last bit of the day. Kasandra hurried herself to the kingdom. The afternoon air shone on her fluttering wings as she flew through the forest towards the castle. Her wings stretched out and flapped as she drifted to the sealed gate. She took out her sword and ran it up against the gate as she flew over.

'Halt! Who goes there?' shouted Cedric, raising his spear.

A banging of metal was heard against the huge wooden gate. It disappeared for a brief moment and a faery appeared over the gate.

'Wait! You cannot enter the castle without permission!'

'Oh yes I can,' said Kasandra.

She fluttered around Cedric, teasing him, before landing next to him, looking up at him. She was about half his height.

'Who ordered your arrival?' questioned Cedric.

Kasandra smiled and leant slowly against the side of his leg. She then extended her wings and rose until her face was level with his.

'Don't worry, love. The king and queen sent for me. Look right here in my hands, a letter from them.'

Cedric immediately noticed the golden parchment in her hands, and stood up straight pulling the spear to his side. He saluted her and looked straight ahead.

'I don't think you want to make me angry now, do you?'

'No, Miss. Um, please, we do not want that.'

Cedric stood very still.

The Silvercrown faeries were magical in their own way.

It was known to the rest of the kingdom that they were indeed different to any other kind of faery, not just because of their ferocity in battle, but because they could do one thing that any other faeries could not: the angrier they got, the bigger they became. Faeries in general were small people, about two-thirds the size of a human. But at their happiest, they could be as short as your arm.

'So, guard. Which way is it, then?'

'Miss, if you please, follow those steps up to the balcony. I believe you will find them there,' he said nervously.

'You are too sweet,' she said with a smirk. She ran her finger down the side of his face and patted him gently on the side of his cheek.

She flew up the stairs and into the balcony room, where she landed softly. She looked around the room and noticed Jargo looking at her.

'See something you like?' she asked.

King Sorbus stood up and smiled towards her.

'Aah. You must be from Silvercrown. I am King Sorbus. It is nice to make your acquaintance.'

She walked up to him and extended her hand in greeting.

'Hello, King Sorbus. I am Kasandra and I am here to represent the Silvercrown faeries. I am a warrior faery.'

'Aren't you a bit small to be a warrior?' questioned Dekrin. He still sat quietly in the corner.

She glared at him.

'For you information, size does not matter in our parts, but it seems to matter here, since you are forced to sit in a corner.'

'For *your* information, I find it rather comfortable sitting here. It gives me a good perspective on things,' retorted Dekrin.

The queen rose and waved her hand. Everyone in the room stood still and kept quiet.

'Before we continue, we need to wait for the representative of one more important village. We are missing someone from the gnome community.'

'Over here,' said a voice from the other end of the table.

'Who said that?' asked Clannk.

Clannk felt a slight tap on his leg. He looked down and noticed a small gnome standing next to him. Grumblestumps looked up at him and tipped his glasses in a kind gesture.

The queen opened her arms and walked over to Grumblestumps.

'It's so good to see you have arrived. We thought you had not made it. We know how busy you are.'

'Mother Queen, once I received the golden parchment I came as quickly as my little legs would allow me,' he said as he looked at them.

King Sorbus invited everyone to sit. Kasandra and Grumblestumps' heads were barely visible above the table. Clannk was big enough to sit on two chairs and sat on one side. Jargo took a comfortable place next to Clannk and folded his hands onto the table's surface. Grumble and Kasandra fumbled in their seats, trying to get comfortable. Two servants entered the room with a pile of cushions.

'I think these might help you,' King Sorbus offered.

'That they will, thank you,' replied Grumble.

'Yeah, thanks.' Kasandra flew and hovered above the chair while the servant placed a few cushions down.

The servants ushered Dekrin from the corner to the end of the table, very carefully. They removed the seats on the end so he could sit without breaking anything.

'Good. Now that everyone is seated, we may start,' said King Sorbus.

'The reason why we called out to the kingdom, well ...'
The queen paused and shook her head.

King Sorbus put his hand on hers and squeezed it.

'What the queen is trying to say is that she has lost her
Marbles.'

Kasandra looked a bit perplexed. She was not sure
whether he was trying to make a joke. She looked at Jargo,
then back at Grumblestumps, for confirmation.

King Sorbus continued.

'I see some confusion in a few of your faces, but for
those who do not know, the Marbles effectively run the
kingdom.'

Dekrin shuffled slightly and stood up.

'You mean you do not run this kingdom and some
Marbles do?' he questioned.

'Well, it is not as simple as that,' the king replied.

Jargo raised his hand.

'If I may interject, Your Highness.'

He turned towards the others and spoke.

'What the king is trying to say is that the balance of this
kingdom in which we continue to exist is governed by the
eternal equilibrium of these metabolic beings captured in
a sphere. Without it, the balance of our universe will cease
to exist.'

The queen pointed at Jargo.

'Exactly. Exactly, what he said,' she said, shaken.

Grumblestumps stood up in his chair, carefully
balancing on the cushions.

'If I may add, in layman's terms, is that if we do not
find these spheres and put them in their rightful place,
we may cease to exist tomorrow. Something of cataclysmic
proportions might occur.'

BLAM!

Grumblestump slammed his fist down on the table. Everyone jumped.

Jargo got up from his chair and circled the long table. He played with his beard for a bit and said, 'How did these Marbles happen to get lost?'

King Sorbus looked carefully around the room and replied, 'Well, for one thing, we are not actually sure. As you know, having served our kingdom for many a century, we keep them locked up!'

Clannk fiddled with his fingers. It kept him from falling asleep. He did not understand what was being said, but knew it was getting late as his stomach was starting to rumble.

The queen opened her mouth and licked her lips.

'We never ever thought someone would be so daring, or stupid, to want to steal the Marbles. Why, on the kingdom's green ground, would anyone want to do this?'

'Power?' asked Kasandra.

'Maybe greed,' said Grumblestumps.

'Money,' thought Jargo out loud.

'Food,' said Clannk.

They all looked at him.

'I'm hungry. Food be nice. Stomach moaning,' he said.

King Sorbus rang the bell he pulled out of his shirt pocket, and called out to the servants to bring refreshments.

Clannk sat up in his chair and smiled.

Dekrin tapped his finger on the ground.

'I think it's all of the above. Some greedy person wanting money and power.'

'I do agree with the young dragon. We have considered that it might be our foes who promised never to cause any chaos again,' said King Sorbus.

'Do you think this might be some retaliation from the

fire goblins after what happened so many years ago?' asked Jargo

'Well, it stands to reason, as I doubt the ogres would want to start any type of war with us.'

The queen stood up and walked to the window. She put both hands on the sill and sighed.

'I want my Marbles back!' she moaned, as tears started to fall from her eyes.

Grumble jumped to the ground and stood beside her. 'I will go in search of the missing marbles. If anything, I might have a good idea of where to start.' He yanked at the side of her dress.

'Whoaa, if there is anyone who should be going it, it is me,' said Jargo.

Dekrin walked over to Jargo, his big feet bashing the floor. 'Who do you think you are, Jargo? King Sorbus, I think I should go. I am big, powerful. I can intimidate anyone in this lousy kingdom. All men, beasts and beings fear dragons. Let me go!'

A sword flew through the air and stabbed itself into the centre of King Sorbus' chair. Kasandra hovered over the table with her arms folded. 'If you need someone killed, I'd be happy to do it for you. Don't let my size fool you. You know what we are capable of,' she said.

King Sorbus raised his hands. 'Stop!' he shouted. 'Stop this instant. I do not want us fighting about who will go on this quest. If any, it should be our most experienced.' He turned and looked at Jargo.

'Food!' shouted Clannk.

The servants brought in a trolley filled with eats. There was meat, sausage, fruit and cake. Lots of cake. They all paused, then rushed towards the trolley. Clannk pushed the servants out of the way and headed straight for the cake.

'Mmmm. Cake good,' he said.

They all stood munching on a piece of delight as King Sorbus turned to the queen and whispered in her ear. 'What shall we do? We can't just choose one. It will make the others mad. You know who my favourite is.'

'Well, I agree. We should show how to keep equilibrium within this kingdom, even if we only do so inside our own balcony room. I suggest we offer a reward to all of them. Whoever brings back the Marbles will be rewarded with whatever they desire.'

King Sorbus thought about what she had said for a moment. He nodded in agreement.

'Let it be done. I think we will have a better chance of succeeding if they all go together. At least we have a one-in-five shot.'

Mother Queen smiled at King Sorbus and laid her hand on his shoulder. King Sorbus walked over to them and watched them guzzle the last bits of food and drink from the trolley.

'The kingdom has come to an agreement. We shall be sending you all on this quest!' he proclaimed.

Jargo spat out some of his cake.

'*All* of us?' he said.

'Excellent! I will show you how to take out a villain,' said Kasandra as she pulled her sword out of the chair.

'Agreed, we will all join forces to find out who did this to the kingdom,' Grumblestumps intoned.

Dekrin swung his tail in delight.

'Will there be food on this journey?' asked Clannk.

'Loads,' responded Jargo.

King Sorbus hugged his queen tightly and patted her on the head.

'Let us put ourselves in their hands. I know they are not

what we were looking for, but let's pray that these unusual heroes can save our kingdom.'

They all said their farewells to the king and queen, who watched them retrace their steps to the castle gate. King Sorbus held the queen close to him. A mouse ran from a hole in the wall, to pick up some leftovers lying on the floor.

It bit into a piece of sausage.

It choked and sneezed.

The piece went flying across the room.

Chapter 7

Goblin City

Some questions are best not discussed around friends, let alone strangers. Yet the questions hung like a silence over the warriors. There were as many pauses in their stunted conversation as there were steps on their journey.

'Nice day, isn't it?' asked Kasandra innocently.

'Rather,' commented Grumblestumps.

'Suppose,' mumbled Clannk.

Jargo looked up at the trees as they stood guard along the stony path. The wind blew gently through their branches. He heard a louder rustle. Kasandra saw him looking up, and her face opened up into a smile. She marched up to him and tapped him on the shoulder with her gleaming sword.

'What's up?'

Jargo looked around, then down at her. He scratched the side of his head and looked all around him.

'Strange feeling, like someone is watching us. Someone lurking in the trees above.'

Kasandra turned and walked over to Grumblestumps.

She stood a little taller than he did. She was not sure whether to trouble his serious thoughts.

'What's your name, Stout?' she asked Grumblestumps.

'My name is Grumblestumps, and I am from the town of Slimpills.'

'I've heard of it. It is right next to ours, yet I've never noticed your kind anywhere before.'

'Our kind?' Grumblestump frowned.

'Yes. You know, the short kind.'

'Well, you're not much taller.'

'Well, um, yes. Do you know where we are heading? I mean, does anyone have an idea of what or who we are supposed to be finding?' she said, shaking her arm above her head.

Jargo took his eyes off the treetops for a moment. He stopped in his tracks and put his hand up.

'If I may stop us right here. I concur that we should come to a consensus about what we want to achieve. We all simply accepted to fight for the king and queen's cause. And that was that. So what do you propose we all *do*? It seems we are all here for very different reasons.'

They all looked at each other and nodded in agreement. Some knew they were walking down a treacherous road that could lead to an unfavourable outcome.

Grumblestumps rubbed his beard. 'From what I can read from everyone's expressions, we all have some pride in ourselves and wish to prove the point that we are the right ones for the job. But I do not think that, if we all investigate at our own pace, we will accomplish anything. I propose we put our differences aside and form some sort of team. We should all take a moment to discuss what value we have in this team. I think that once we understand what each other's capabilities are, we could come up with a strategy.'

Jargo again nodded his head in agreement. 'I agree,

Grumblestumps. I think we should all take a moment to say what strengths we have. I would like to start, if I may.'

The five beings formed a semicircle around Jargo and listened intently.

'Well, as you might have heard from King Sorbus, I served the kingdom for many years, but I am now retired to the Palace of Elders, and...'

'Ooooh, I've heard of that place. It's where all the old people go, isn't it?' replied Kasandra.

'Quiet, you. Let him finish. Everyone will have a turn,' mumbled Grumble.

'And, I am a conjurer, something of a sorcerer, if you like. I achieve this through magic and my trusty wand. Like this one.' Jargo pulled from his robe a wooden wand with a pointed end. It was worn where Jargo held it, and the tip looked burnt.

Grumblestumps moved forward into the half-circle and pushed his glasses up his nose.

'I am a medicine gnome. I can create a potion for just about anything.'

He took a few steps back, to the edge of the circle.

Kasandra drew her sword and pegged it into the sand where she stood. She pushed her helmet up so the others could see her eyes. Her wings spread as she flew up to hover above the sword's handle. 'The name's Kasandra. I am a warrior faery. I can fight, and this sword right here can do a lot of damage when I am around.'

Clannk pulled her sword out of the ground with one hand. With the other, he grabbed Kasandra around the waist. 'Me Clannk. Me strong and powerful. Hungry too.'

'Would you mind taking your hand off of me?' Kasandra drew one of her daggers and jammed it into Clannk's hand.

'Ouch!'

He let go of her and she dropped to the ground.

'See, I can defend myself,' Kasandra said smugly.

'Well, that leaves the dragon here. But I am sure we all know what he is capable of. Fire, destruction ...' Jargo said.

Dekrin stood still, watching.

'Well, what Jargo means to say is ... is that I can bring strength and flight to the team.'

Grumblestumps moved towards Dekrin and put his hand on his tail.

'Let me guess ... at your age, I assume you'd have learnt the art of firebreath ... but looking into your eyes, I sense you have not.'

Dekrin pulled his tail away from Grumblestumps' touch. He walked away from the group and leant against a tree. He turned to them and sighed.

'It is not as easy as it looks.'

Kasandra burst out laughing. She rolled on the ground until Clannk pick her up gently again and held her up in the air by her shirt until she calmed down. Jargo folded his arms again and rolled his eyes. 'Oh my. By the powers of the Elders, what have I let myself in for?'

His eyes passed from one warrior to the next. All he saw was a dragon that could not breathe fire; a troll that was hungry all the time; a warrior faery that didn't care about other beings' feelings; and a three-foot gnome that could make you a tasty potion. He buried his face in his hands, then rubbed his eyes in disbelief.

Kasandra stood up, fixed her hair and put her helmet back on. Dekrin turned to the others. 'Let us get serious. We have an idea of what each of us can offer. Now, can any of you offer some insight into where we are going to start our search?'

'Goblin City,' replied Jargo.

'Why Goblin City?' Kasandra asked.

'Let's just call it a hunch,' said Jargo.

Grumblestumps scratched in his bag and pulled out the crooked piece of glass he'd picked up. He held it up for everyone to see. Clannk could not really see despite leaning down, so he picked Grumblestumps up by the waist and lifted the gnome to his face.

'What's that?' he asked Grumblestumps.

'This, my strong fellow, is something I picked up in the woods near our town.'

Jargo waved his wand, and the crooked piece of glass hovered in front of him. He examined it closely for a while. As Clannk slowly lowered Grumble to the ground, Kasandra opened her wings and flew up to see what the object was. She tried to see it from all angles, flying around it in circles.

Dekrin walked up to a nearby tree and scratched his scaly back on it. Some of the leaves showered down. He pretended not to be interested in everyone's business.

An ugly figure closed his hand into a fist. He opened it, then pointed his finger and stared at it. His eye watched it move from side to side as a hook picked under its nail.

Glasshook watched the flickering light bounce off his hand as he sat solemnly in his awkward wooden chair. It was held together with a few bent nails and round pieces of hardened bark. He sucked on his tooth and spat on the ground beside his chair.

'Where is Blister?' he boomed.

A figure skipped from one foot to the other around the corner.

'Oh Master. He is on his way,' Cracker sang. He bowed before Glasshook, stooping beyond his short, dirty trousers to his badly worn leather shoes.

'Where are the others?' asked Glasshook.

To the side of the large dark room, a door opened. Two

goblins carried a very heavy chest with a rusted lock through it. They placed it in front of Glasshook with a thunk. 'With bounty we come to you. Handing you treasure, this is true,' the goblins sang. Glasshook's minions were a cheerful bunch, singing everything they said.

Blister was the leader of the minions, since Glasshook had given him the right to think for the others. The minions were happy with this, as it gave them more time to be cheerful and to sing. Cracker stood up straight and waved his hands towards Shiftface and Pile. He waved them closer. They skipped up to his side and grabbed each other by the waist, laughing and singing:

> *Blister is our Mister,*
> *Our leader, if you must.*
> *The one we enter battle with,*
> *In whom we place our trust.*
> *We bring you jewels to light the sky!*
> *Diamonds this big you cannot deny!*
> *So let us share this treasure,*
> *We will be rich forever!*

The three minions cheered and snickered as Blister entered with a cartwheel and a back-flip that stretched his tattered waistcoat and short shorts. His acrobatics caused his gold earrings to glitter in the low light.

'Master! Master! We minions bring you delights, to brighten your nights!' he said gleefully to Glasshook, who sat back in his chair, crossed his legs, pointed to the chest with his hook and commanded Blister to open it.

'It will be our pleasure to open up this treasure!' the minions sang together.

Pile grabbed the lock and shook it a few times. Shiftface

pushed him to one side and pulled a large hammer from his pants, shouting 'It's hammer time!'

He started to bash the living daylights of the chest and giggled between every strike.

'Another! Another!' the three goblins bellowed.

The lock surrendered, breaking into little pieces. Some dust settled back onto the punished chest as the shouts died down.

'Are they in there?' asked Glasshook, gruff and impatient.

'They are, all of them, by far!'

'Open the chest. Slowly.'

Blister took the end of the lid and pushed it up very slowly. A blinding light forced itself through the opening. The light was so magnificent that it instantly lit up the entire room.

'Shut it!' yelled Glasshook, lurching forward to slam the lid shut with his hook. Seconds later, his laughter rose into the dank air. The minions joined him; Pile laughed so much he fell to the floor.

Grumblestumps closed his hand around the piece of glass, slipping it back into his leather pouch. He pressed his glasses back up his nose. Jargo glanced at the skies and urged the small band to move on. The day was wearing on. If they wanted to find Goblin City, they would need to make progress before darkness took over the woods. The five reached the other side of the forest to find a stony path.

'Is this the way?' asked Kasandra.

'It is. Now let's move,' replied Jargo.

Dekrin took flight above them and circled the air for a while. Clannk watched him lazily. He had never seen a real dragon before, and the sight of one in flight made him smile. He began to think that there was more to life than enjoying a good piece of pie. He tugged at the rope that kept his pants up as Jargo noticed a line of smoke in the distant sky. He knew they were not too far away.

'Not far now,' he announced to the others.

'Good. Hungry,' moaned Clannk.

Jargo whipped out his wand and waved it in the air. 'May mushrooms be your delight,' he intoned. Right in front of Clannk, a huge mound of Shwarmi Mushrooms formed. Clannk bent down and picked as many as his hands could carry. He started to munch on them straight away. 'My goodness!' How did you manage that?' asked Grumble. Jargo smiled. 'It is a command I learnt many moons ago. I understand these mushrooms are of the rare type, but in this particular part of the woods, you will find many fungi.'

'Aah, I see.' Grumble picked up a few and stuffed them into his potion bag.

'Do remember, Clannk. Don't eat too many of them. They can lead to loss of sensation in the mouth.' 'Mmmmw HUH?' Clannk replied, with a mouthful of mushrooms.

A wind picked up around them as Dekrin landed. He ran up to Jargo's side and nudged him with his nose. 'I assume up ahead is Goblin City? I see lots of smoke coming from it. What are they cooking up in there?'

'Dragon brains!' Kasandra laughed. 'They love dragon brains; they say they give goblins eternal life. So you'd best watch out.'

Dekrin turned to Jargo nervously. 'That can't be true, can it? I mean, I am not *that* clever. I mean, my brain wouldn't make them anymore life-like.'

Jargo patted the dragon's side. 'Fear not, she is just pulling your tail. If anything, it's the dragon's breath that can give life to the eternal mind. And since you have not yet mastered it, we need not worry.'

The dragon looked down the path and frowned, unsure

of what lay ahead, but proceeded to follow the others carefully. Burnt stumps marked their approach to the gates of Goblin City. In the distance, a high metal frame with burnt pieces of wood imitated a gate. Rusty chains hung from its sides. Two barrels blazed with open fire on each side. The smoke billowed from the dancing flames. Huge sharpened logs pointed at the hazy skyline. A tall lookout post stood high above the gate, from which a long horn hung. Two goblins kept watch.

The five heroes approached the gates cautiously. A voice rang out over the crackling of fire, booming through the curved brown horn: 'Goblin City smells so pretty. Who goes there?' Jargo took a step forward but was stopped by Kasandra's sword across his chest.

'I will handle this,' she said confidently. She took flight, soaring up to the tower.

'You are too close! We will not mind to hurt you most,' the guard cautioned. She landed between the two guards. They both stood very still as she held her sword to one of their throats.

'Right. It would be very kind of you to allow us to enter your city,' she said menacingly.

The other guard moved slowly toward the ladder to escape. But Kasandra pulled out one of her daggers and pinned him up against the side of the tower. 'You are not going anywhere. And as for you, I think it would be best that you open up this gate for your guests.' She leant up hard against him and slowly started to grow bigger in size. 'I don't think you want me to get angry now, do you?'

The guard's hand shook as it carefully grabbed the end of the horn.

'That's it. Now, very slowly, and in your best voice, get them to open the gates for us.' She grabbed his ear and pulled it slightly. Standing back, she lowered her sword to his waist and held it there.

A voice boomed over the horn and echoed through the forests.

'Open the gate, to enter is at your own fate.'

'Why thank you, kind goblin. Today you will live to tell your tale.'

She took off and flew back to where the others watched from below.

The others looked at her as she stood in front of them with her arms folded.

'Whenever you are ready,' she smirked.

Grumblestumps walked passed her and patted her on the shoulder. Jargo took the lead and asked the others to follow swiftly.

'Just remember, eyes straight, don't stare at any of them. That is what they want, so don't allow yourself to fall under the spell of their evil smiles.'

The gates opened slowly with a strain of a huge rusty chain. Two chains hung from the gate and five goblins pulled on each one as it swung open.

The goblins sung out words to each pull.

'Pull you fool. Pull you fool.'

Clannk stared at them as he wandered passed. A tail met the side of his rear. Dekrin reminded to him not to stare.

Inside the wooden walls, waste metal lay everywhere. Piles of dirty burning wood and several lame attempts at huts littered the ground. Goblins pilfered the rubbish in search of any treasures they could lay their dirty hands on. On the far side of the city, a large structure resembled a house.

Jargo pointed to a goblin who sat outside of the house playing with a jewel. 'Where is he?'

'You seek the freak?'

'Yes.'

'Inside he will not hide,' said the goblin.

Jargo walked up the steps and entered the house. The others followed him one by one. Dekrin had to lower his head. The house was dark, with only a few slivers of light entering through cracks in the walls. A few ugly candles lay in the corners. The candles shed enough light to show a chair and someone sitting in it. Jargo cautioned everyone to stand still. Kasandra walked up to him and looked at the being sitting quietly in the chair. The goblin moved forward and leant on his left arm.

'Can I help you?' it said.

'What's with the hand, ugly?' Kasandra pointed to the glass hook.

Jargo pushed Kasandra out of the way and spoke.

'Glasshook.'

'*You*! What are *you* doing here? How did you get into the City?' he demanded.

Kasandra grew a little taller and stepped forward.

'Well, if you must know, I had something to do with that. Let us just say I am a bit more convincing than others. Oh, and your guards are *such* a delight.'

'We have come to ask you a few questions, Glasshook,' said Jargo.

'And what questions do you honestly think I would answer?'

Grumblestumps turned to Jargo and looked up at him. Their eyes turned back towards Glasshook.

'With your history, I assume you would be the one in a position to help provide some answers for me.'

'And what makes your think I would provide them to you?' Glasshook continued to lean on his hook with his chin.

'Well, it is for the kingdom's sake, and given what you

did to it last time, I think you owe yourself an opportunity to answer.'

Glasshook stood up from his chair and pointed his hook at Jargo.

'After what you have done to me?' he shouted.

Kasandra held Grumblestumps' shoulder and whispered. 'So what did he do? Paint an uglier picture of him? You can't get any uglier than that!' as she pointed towards the goblin.

'I am not sure myself.'

Jargo took a step forward and crossed his arms, his wand still in his hand.

'Look. I am sure you know why we are here. So just tell me what I need to know and we will be off.'

The goblin held his hands behind his back and walked around his chair. He stopped and turned to face the others.

'Nothing in this life of ours is for free. It is all about gain. If you want to gain information, what do I gain?'

Jargo straightened his arms at his sides.

'Your life.'

Glasshook laughed out loud. He could not believe his ears.

'Let us cut to the chase, Jargo. I heard a Wallow-shriek Bird say that the kingdom is in a bit of a bind. And some information has come my way that might interest you.'

'But at a price, I gather?' the wizard answered.

'Yes. At a price. I know how valuable this information is to you. And who are these with you? Your followers? Let me remind you, Jargo is no man to follow. Chaos always seems to find him. You'd best be aware. If I were you, I would just go back to your villages. Oh, and since when did you need any help, Jargo?' Glasshook asked.

'The kingdom insisted.'

Clannk slammed his fist into his hand.

'We want you to tell.'

Kasandra flew up into the air. 'Yes, before us warriors here cut you a new hole for an earring.'

Glasshook laughed again and sat back in his chair.

'Then you know what I want in return.'

Jargo looked at the warriors before he answered.

'You know I cannot give it back. You know the rules.'

Dekrin had a very puzzled look on his face. He was not certain of the rules. He assumed it was because he was still young and had not been taught them.

'What rules are these?' Dekrin asked.

Glasshook scratched his tooth with his hook and smiled.

Jargo opened his mouth to speak. 'Glasshook and I have walked a very long road together. Remember the Tirade of the Fire Globins? Glasshook here is the one who sparked the whole attack on the kingdom. So, for his efforts, the rules of the kingdom were composed. According to them, whoever chooses to fight against the kingdom and loses has to sacrifice something he truly loves.'

Glasshook raised his hand.

Dekrin thought he knew the answer. 'Did you have to sacrifice all your gold and jewels? Goblins are greedy for jewels.'

'Indeed we are, but they took more than just my jewels. They took the one thing from me that I can use to gain jewels.'

'His hand,' said Jargo, and looked down at the floor.

'YES! MY HAND! You see this? This glass hook is now my hand. What can a goblin do without both hands? NOTHING!' he shouted.

'No one can ever replace his hand. No magic will do this for him. He knows the rules.'

Grumblestumps grabbed his potion bag and rumbled through it. He pulled out his potion book and flipped through it a few times.

'Aha!'

'What you got?' asked Clannk.

'I have found something that might do the trick.'

Grumblestumps forced his way through everyone and walked up to where the goblin sat. He raised his hand and cleared his throat.

'Mr. Glasshook. I have something that may interest you.'

'And what is it, shrimp?' the goblin snarled.

'I come from the town called Slimpills, and through the generations we have studied medicine. I have been handed down a recipe for a potion that will indeed grow your hand back.'

Glasshook immediately sat up.

'What do you mean? Grow back?'

'Uh, yes. Grow back. See, potions are often in liquid form. For them to work, you will have to ingest a concoction I will make.'

'Is this true?' Glasshook looked back at Jargo.

Before Jargo could say anything he was stopped by a quick wink from Grumblestump.

'I am not familiar with gnome potions, but I will allow Grumblestumps to continue,' the wizard said.

The other three warriors stood and watched Grumble explain.

'Good. I will prepare this potion right away. The only thing I need is some hair from you.'

Glasshook felt his head a few times with his hand.

'I have no hair. Goblins have no hair.'

'Such a shame.'

'Wait! If you really think this will work, I will give you the answer you seek.'

'Well then, I need something from you. How about a nail?'

Glasshook looked at his finger and then proceeded to put it in his mouth. He took one hard bite at his pointy nail and tore off a piece with his teeth. The piece of nail flew from his mouth as he spat it onto the floor. Grumble bent over and picked up the sticky piece and put it in a glass jar. He fumbled through his bag for a few more ingredients, Shwarmi mushrooms being one of them.

He moved to the side of everyone, and crouched down to dig into his pouch. He pulled out a cloth, which he laid down on the floor. He grabbed a piece of the mushroom, nail, and a few other items he produced from his bag. He put them into the jar, and added some liquid from a bottle he had tucked away in his waistcoat. He shook the mixture vigorously until the substance turned purple. He opened the top of the jar ; he pulled his head to the side as he twisted the cap. It oozed a yellow smoke that floated up towards the roof.

'Eew, it stinks!' said Kasandra, holding her nose.

Grumble closed the lid and threw the jar into the air. It flipped over several times, then landed safely back into Grumble's hand. The liquid in the jar immediately turned clear.

'Aah. I think it is ready,' he said.

Glasshook stood up from the chair and walked over to him.

'Give me that!' he demanded.

'You promise to give us an answer?' Jargo replied.

'Yes! Just give me the potion!'

Glasshook grabbed the jar from Grumble's small hand and twisted open the cap. He sniffed the potion first and smiled to everyone. He raised the jar as if making a toast, and said, 'Here is to success, honesty and greed.' He gulped down the potion in one draw, then threw the jar against the wall. It smashed into tiny pieces on the floor.

His eyes fixated on his glass hook. He held it up towards the roof. Everyone watched him walk in circles around the room.

'The room is spinning. What did you give me? Did you poison me, you dwarf?'

Grumble cleared his throat and said, 'It's gnome, and no, I did not poison you. A slight side effect from the potion, it seems.'

Glasshook grasped his left arm tightly and held the hook closely to his face. What looked like terror in his eye was soon overcome by a huge smile.

'I see it! I SEE IT!' Look, it has begun!'

The heroes stared at him and stared at each other. They were not sure what to make of what was happening.

'Hahahahahahahah!' the goblin laughed out hysterically.

'Finally, I have my way. You will not regret this.'

Glasshook could not take his eyes off his hand. He held it with his right tightly.

'It is growing. Look!'

Kasandra started to open her mouth, but a hand quickly covered it. Grumblestumps urged her to refrain from saying anything. The wizard pointed his wand towards the twirling goblin.

'You have got what you wanted. Now give us what we need!' he ordered.

'All mine and you cannot take it away!' the goblin screamed.

The others noticed that Jargo had lost patience with

the goblin; they watched him raise his wand towards Glasshook.

'Glasshook! Give us the answer we seek!'

The goblin stopped and stared into the corner. He raised both his hands in the shape of fists. He turned his face to look over his shoulder; some of the outside light fell onto his eyes. He smirked, and pointed towards the door.

'The answer you seek is ... Wurken Gerkin.'

With one flick of his wand, Jargo vanished, leaving nothing but dust where the heroes stood moments before.

Chapter 8

Ogreville

To lie is to cheat. Yet situations sometimes required one either to lie or to cheat. This one required both. If the outcome was favourable, who would complain? Only those who gained nothing from it.

A cloud of dust circled the grassy field. It swept up like a tornado, then stopped suddenly. Five creatures appeared, all of them bewildered, except for one. Jargo dusted himself off with his hat. He smiled and wiped his brow.

'That was a close one!' he remarked.

'Close one? What?' said Dekrin.

'I mean, there stood Glasshook, mad as a fox, and the next moment we are standing here, all feeling a bit delirious.'

There were times when foxes ran around in the forests surrounding the kingdom as if they had a race to win. They would dash around from tree to tree, almost hiding behind each one for a moment. Most forest dwellers were not sure what they were looking for. Some said they were looking for their sanity.

Grumblestumps picked himself from the ground, walked around in a circle and looked towards the skies. He was trying to familiarise himself with his surroundings, but failed to recognise where he was. Kasandra noticed the confusion on everyone's faces except Jargo's.

She pulled out her sharp-edged sword and pointed it at Jargo.

'Now, you'd better tell me how we got here!' she said, menacingly.

Jargo pushed her sword away from his knee with his hand.

'Don't go making me mad now. You do not want me to be looking into your eyes right now.'

Dekrin flexed his wings and smiled.

'Now that is what I would like to see.'

'Big Kas. Big, big Kas.' Clannk added.

The wizard threw his hands into the air. Everyone looked attentively at him.

'Alright. If you must know. The thing is, you do not know what Glasshook is capable of. I simply took a decision on behalf of everyone here, and got us the HELL out of Goblin City.'

Dekrin leaned towards Jargo and stared into his blinking eyes. He snarled and showed his dagger-like teeth.

'I think we can take care of ourselves. Well, especially me!' he snorted.

A little body pushed its way forward and in between the two.

Grumblestumps looked up at the dragon and waved his finger at him.

'May I intervene please? I do believe a choice had to be made at that instant.'

'And what choice would that be?' asked Kasandra.

Clannk looked for a place to sit down and found a flat rock nearby. He walked over and picked it up easily with both hands, then carried it to where the discussion was happening. The boulder thumped onto the ground as it left his oversized hands. He sat down clumsily onto it. He pulled a piece of dry grass from the ground and merrily started to suck on it.

The wizard rubbed his beard with his right hand.

'Jargo is right.' said Grumblestumps. 'He had to get us out there as quickly as possible. Glasshook would soon have realised what had been done, and we would have been done for!'

Kasandra looked very confused. She looked up at Dekrin for insight, but he just shrugged his leathery wings and stared back at the wizard.

'Done for? What do you mean? I thought you gave him what he wanted and in return gave us what we wanted?'

'Working Birdpin?' mumbled Clannk.

'No! It's Wurken Gerkin,' Kasandra said, irritated.

Grumblestumps put his finger onto his mouth and cautioned Kasandra to keep quiet for a brief moment so he could explain.

'As I said before, Jargo is right. When someone brings harm and chaos to the kingdom, he or she will be punished under the King's Law. And this Law says, he or she who sacrifices the harmony of the kingdom for personal gain will sacrifice their own harmony.'

The dragon turned his head away and sat down next to the troll, who innocently gazed at the surroundings.

Jargo stepped forward, adding, 'Yes. Glasshook causing the tirade against the kingdom had to make a sacrifice, so we took away something that could not be given back. And as you know, this was his hand.'

'But why was he on about seeing his hand growing back? I thought you said no magic in the entire kingdom could bring it back? So how was Grumblestumps able to give it back to him?' questioned Kasandra.

Grumblestumps smiled at her. He took her by the hand and placed a stone into it. She looked down at it, and then back at him.

'What do you see?'

'A stupid piece of rock,' she said, sarcastically.

'Ah, a piece of rock to you, maybe. But to another, it might be a flower.'

Clannk shifted in his stony seat to have a better look at what was in her hand.

'Looks like a stone,' he said.

'Yes, but with some help from a potion, an elixir, or a forest juice, you can imagine it to be anything you want it to be.'

'You mean a hallucination made him see his hand grow?' frowned Kasandra.

Jargo carefully took his spiral wand out and flicked it.

Kasandra looked down at her hand and saw a green centipede wriggling around.

'Gross!' she screamed, dropping the centipede onto the ground.

They all laughed out loud.

'That was not funny!'

Dekrin whispered to Clannk, 'Girls will be girls.'

Grumblestumps wiped his eyes and cleared his throat.

'The potion I made had one very important ingredient in it. The Shwarmi Mushroom. It is tremendously versatile. Different quantities in a potion produce different effects. In this case, one third of the mushroom produced what I like to call the Imaginarium Effect.'

'Imagina ... na ... na? stuttered Clannk.

'Imaginarium Effect,' corrected Kasandra.

'This effect is not a hallucination, but stirs your senses into believing what it wants you to believe.'

Jargo interrupted the conversation with a cough.

'So Glasshook really believed his hand was growing? It was really all in his head?'

Grumbles nodded his head at Jargo.

'Yes indeed. It was all in his imagination. The Imaginarium Effect.'

'Aaaaah.'

Everyone understood and nodded their heads in agreement.

'How long does it last?' asked Clannk.

'Only for a short while. It can last a little longer, depending on how strong the being's imagination is. In Glasshook's case, I am sure we had a few minutes more. But I am glad Jargo took us away in time. Who knows what would have happened when he realised what I had done.'

Dekrin stood up and stretched his wings. It caused a bit of a breeze, which soon settled once he stopped flapping.

'I guess we can safely say the goblin fell for it hook, line and sinker.'

They all laughed again.

The wind stiffened among the trees, which shook their leaves. They all looked up at the ruffling. Their eyes met again briefly, before Dekrin broke the silence.

'So, where are we exactly, Jargo?' asked Dekrin.

'I, um, am actually not sure. When a wizard uses this particular spell, he has to announce his destination. I think I might have left that part out.'

Clannk looked down at his grumbling stomach and rubbed it.

'Oh my,' said Grumblestumps.

'Well, to be honest, all I had on my mind was getting us out of there as quickly as possible.'

Dekrin searched the nearby clearing for any clues about where they were. Grumblestumps walked a little way up a meandering footpath. He focused for a moment before he turned towards the others. He crossed his hands behind him and rocked back and forth on his tip toes.

'The answer to where we are is only relevant to the question of where we are headed,' he remarked.

Clannk's eyes never left his growling stomach, but his mouth threw out a thought.

'Um, does anyone know what or where the Working Turkpin is?'

A few blank faces responded to his question, except one.

Kasandra peered up towards a distant mountain sticking its lazy head above the trees.

'You mean the Wurken Gerkin. And, well, maybe I do.'

Everyone stood with their mouths open and stared at her.

'Now why would you know what or where this could possibly be?' Grumblestumps questioned doubtfully.

Kasandra had led a particularly misleading life. She grew up in a family of proud fighters for the Silvercrown faeries. They were revered for their loyalty and honour in keeping peace within their sanctuary. However, the disappointment always hung over her head for being the only daughter to a successful fighter. It led her to rebel against her father, who never saw her to be anything other than a girl. Over the years, as she aged, she became increasingly reckless. She found her enjoyment in places where no one cared who or what you were, as long as you could drink like a fish and dance like you were on walking on glass with oily feet.

She could do both, without spilling a drop from her mug. These hideouts, lost homes and bars were spread out across all corners of the kingdom. They were best left at these far corners, so as not to overshadow the kingdom's glorious reputation. Kasandra had frequented them all, to seek the acceptance from others that she'd never received from her family and home. These were the only places she could be herself, and some even looked up to her. Or, in her small case, looked down at her a little less.

Kasandra put her hands on her hips and breathed out.

'I know where it is, because I have been there. Several times.'

Clannk pushed himself up with his right hand and stretched.

'Let's go, then,' he said.

Everyone peered at him.

'To the Wurken Gerkin.' Clannk added.

'It's *Wurken Gerkin*!' said Kasandra, in a bit of a huff. 'Oh wait – you *did* say Wurken Gerkin. Who would have thought?'

Jargo smiled at Grumblestumps, and nodded his head.

Dekrin pushed his way through the centre of the discussion and turned to the rest.

'So what are we waiting for? Point me in the direction and I will fly us there. That is, of course, if everyone would prefer to take the long way around. I like to travel by air – there is far less traffic to avoid.'

Jargo shifted on the spot. He scratched his head with his wand.

'No offence, my dragon. But I would prefer to get there by my own means.'

Dekrin smiled and snorted.

'None taken. Although I would like to get there on my own steam. My wings need a good stretching.'

'Who would like to travel with the dragon, and who would like to come with me?'

The curiosity of a gnome had always been immense. And with Grumblestumps, it was no different.

'If there are no objections, I would like to keep the young dragon company. I suggest the rest of you travel with the wizard.'

Everyone nodded in approval. The dragon lay flat down on his belly and extended his front leg. Grumblestumps grabbed onto a clawed finger and hoisted himself up. The dragon gently raised him up onto his back. Grumblestumps got comfortable between the horns that stuck in out in different lengths. He pulled out some rope he had in his bag of potions and secured it around one of the horns. He tied the other end around his waist.

Dekrin looked back at the gnome, disapproving.

'This is my first flight on the back of a dragon, and I wish to have a safe one.'

'One more thing, Kasandra. Could you kindly point in the direction of this Wurken Gerkin place?' asked Dekrin.

The faery stood and looked up towards the mountain top.

'It is on the edge of Ogreville. There is a winding path through a clearing and you pass around the west side of that mountain top. You will see it as soon as you come over the edge. There is always smoke streaming out of the building. You should be able to see it for miles.'

Grumblestumps shifted slightly and grabbed on tightly to the rope he had around him. He tapped the dragon on his back of his neck.

'Ready when you are.'

'Oh, I am so ready!' shouted Dekrin. He immediately took flight and did a few twists and circles in the sky before waving the others goodbye.

'Oh dear,' moaned Grumblestumps, and held on for his life.

Jargo looked at the other two and waved them to come closer.

'It looks like it's just us. If you don't mind, you need to stand a bit closer, so I can move us all in one piece.'

'One piece?' asked Clannk.

'Yes, if you are not within the circle, parts of you might be left behind. And I do not think it will be too comfortable when we get to the other side.'

Kasandra and Clannk both rushed to either side of Jargo. Clannk grabbed Jargo around the shoulders and squeezed him tightly.

With the wizard squashed up against the big frame of the troll, he mumbled. 'I do not think we need to be *this* close.'

'Me don't want to leave anything behind,' Clannk said nervously.

Kasandra adjusted her sword belt and ran her fingers through her messy hair. She grabbed the side of Jargo's dark robe and held on tightly. Her eyes shut as she stood motionless. Jargo nodded his head at Clannk and looked down at the faery.

He took out his wand and pointed it at the mountain top. A light streamed out the tip of his wand.

'Places where we want to be.'

BANG!

A cloud of dust rose and settled on the forest floor.

On the edge of a winding path lay a dreary old house. A cracked, dirty window sat beside a blackened, knotted door in the middle of the front of the house. A huge pile of wood leant up against one side of the house. The pile stood taller than the roof. A sign swung lazily next to the door:

Wurken Gerkin – Enter at ye own peril

Smoke billowed from a stone chimney, standing tall above the house. There were broken tiles on the roof, and some lay scattered on the ground. The place was a real mess, yet it buzzed with activity. In the far distance stood Ogreville, with the Wurken Gerkin on its outskirts – there simply because ogres loved to drink. Their fondness for drinking too much, and for fighting among themselves when they'd overindulged, made it difficult to have the tavern in the village. Competition between ogres was fierce and many a challenge would be laid down to establish superiority. These challenges often involved destruction; the village did not appreciate the fact that each passing day resulted in a little less of the village remaining intact. So the villagers forced the tavern towards the village outskirts, to give the ogres who dwelled there plenty of time to resolve their differences in the open. After they left the tavern, the walk back to the village was long enough to sober them up. Generally, they were slightly more civil by the time they returned.

The door swung open and Jargo entered first. Clannk followed, ducking slightly under the door frame. The bustling bar went silent. Everyone turned in their chairs and stared towards the entrance. The barman, a burly but short ogre, nodded at them. The door shut. Kasandra stepped out from behind Jargo.

Every face in the room lit up.

'Kasandra!' they all shouted in unison.

'Hi everyone,' she said, embarrassed.

The barman smiled and grabbed a mug from under his counter. He spat into it.

'The usual, my fair lady?' he asked.

'Yes, but with a little less spit this time,' she answered.

Jargo and Clannk stared.

The smell of stale beer, sweat and smoke hung in the air. For most newcomers, this was a smell that took some getting used to. To Kasandra it smelt like home. Jargo leant towards her and whispered, 'I hope you know what you are doing in here. Many of these faces have crossed my path, and I have not approved of many of them.'

She turned to him and smirked.

'Not to worry, I have a good reputation here. Luckily you are part of that. So, sit down and relax. See! Even Clannk is getting in on the act. Just remain calm.'

Clannk pulled up a bar stool and sat down.

'Give me three of your best brews, and whatever you can find to eat,' he said, pointing at the barman.

Next to Clannk sat an enormous muscled ogre. He looked mean, even from behind. He was so big that he took up two seats at the bar. He sat with one hand around a mug of brew and picked his teeth with the other, using what looked like a small tree.

Kasandra dragged a chair to an empty table near the window and sat down. Jargo's eyes roamed the inside and noticed a huge fireplace pushing flames and smoke up into its chimney. Burnt-out candles were scattered around every window sill and table. In one corner lay a very drunk ogre whose snores sounded like he was sawing the logs outside. A few older-looking goblins occupied another table. At the end of the room, a few humans sat in suits of armour. Jargo frowned at them as they glanced in his direction. They quickly turned away, hugged their drinking mugs and looked out the window.

Jargo sat down as the barman came around with two dirty mugs of brew.

'There you go. It's on the house,' the barman said proudly.

Kasandra grabbed his arm and rubbed it. She looked

at him and blinked her eyes. Jargo had never seen an ogre blush before. The beer in front of him looked disgusting, but it smelt good. He took a quick sip. Kasandra picked up her glass and held it above her head.

'It is so good to be back. May I say, here is to many a fortune!'

'Hear, hear!' everyone shouted together as they joined the toast.

Clannk looked over at the bulky Ogre. He noticed that his mug, carved out of wood, was shaped like a goblin's face. 'Nice Mug. Yours?' he asked.

The ogre shifted in his direction and pulled the piece of branch out of his mouth. A piece of meat that had been stuck in between his teeth flew out and hit Jargo in the face. The piece slid slowly down Jargo's cheek and onto his table.

Again everyone went very quiet. Jargo wiped his face with his sleeve.

'Thank you, Ogre. If I indeed needed a piece of meat for a bruised eye, you would have been the first person I would have asked.'

Kasandra looked around the room nervously, and then stood up. She grabbed her mug and laughed.

'Hahahahaha! Good one there, Jargo!' she yelled, and slapped him on his back.

A shuffle of laughter started to echo through the bar. It got louder, and before you could take another sip of your spit brew, everyone was in hysterics.

Behind the bar counter hung a large rusty iron bell. The barman grabbed it and rung it twice.

'For the next hour, drinks are on the house!'

A roar of approvals went up into the air. Some even tossed their mugs and watched them come crashing down onto the dusty floor.

The muscular ogre put his elbow on the counter and leant on it. He took a gulp from his carved mug and burped.

'I haven't seen a troll your size before?' he mumbled.

Clannk looked at himself and then back at the ogre.

'So what do they feed your kind?'

'Hollow pie,' Clannk replied and took another sip of his brew.

Kasandra took flight and sat in between the two at the bar. She crossed her legs and leant back onto her arms. He legs swung over the edge of the counter.

'Brok, I have not had the chance to speak to you lately. How are you doing?'

'Good. What do you want, Kas?'

'Nothing – well, not yet. We hardly chat these days, you being so busy and all, with bounting, that is.'

Ogreville had always bred big ogres; Brok was the largest. He was certainly an abomination. But the older he became the stronger and more dangerous he was to the village. He never lost a fight, and intended never to lose one either. But over time, he started losing his place within the village, and soon became an outcast. This forced him to spend many days in the Wurken Gerkin, drinking his sorrows away. Like many who had visited the bar, he was approached, many years ago, by a traveller. The stranger walked into the bar one day wearing a very long brown cloak. A sword stuck out from the side of the cloak. The man's face was covered by a hood, his chin covered by a beard. It was the only thing visible from under the cloak. The man had sat next to Brok and given him an opportunity to gain riches. He'd offered Brok the lifeline he'd been looking for. A deal was put on the counter, and it was simple. The man would give Brok names written on a piece of parchment, and those whom he could bring back to the bar in one piece would gain him gold. Lots of it. Brok would only meet the stranger for a minute at a time, yet the understanding was complete. Give the man what he wanted and be rewarded. And so it was told over the years how dominant Brok became as the most fearless bounty hunter known to the kingdom.

'Have your muscles got bigger?' asked Kasandra.

'Who are your friends? And what are they doing here?' Kasandra shifted a little closer to Brok.

'We just came for a drink, that's all.'

Brok stood up and bashed down his mug. He looked right down with one eye into Kasandra's eyes. The others around the room just stared into their drinks. The ogre in the corner continued to snore.

Kasandra gazed back up to the brute.

'But I thought we were friends,' she said.

'We are not friends. We tolerate *your* kind in here, but we do not tolerate *his* kind in here!' Brok pointed at the wizard. Jargo took another sip from his mug and looked behind him.

'Oh. You meant me,' he remarked.

'Can't a wizard mind his own business and come in for an honest drink?'

The ogre took a step towards the wizard. He was stopped in his tracks by a pull on his arm. He turned and noticed Clannk that held him tightly.

'I see you're quite strong for a troll. But I suggest you better let go if you want to keep that hand of yours,' he grunted.

'Um, no,' said Clannk.

'You will not be hurting any of my friends.'

The ogre grabbed Clannk by his neck and pushed him heavily up against the bar counter. He squeezed tightly and the troll tried to free himself by pulling with both of his hands. Kasandra stood up onto the counter and drew her sword. She flew up into the air and held it against the ogre's throat.

'I do not think you want to be doing that, Brok,' she said, nicely.

The wizard immediately stood up and knocked over his chair. They all turned in his direction and stared as he stood with his wand out.

'Don't even think about it!' Jargo said forcefully.

Brok broke out into a huge smile. A huge gold tooth flickered against the dim light that shone through the window. The ogre released Clannk's throat and enthusiastically sat him down back on his chair. His hand dusted his shoulders off and patted him on his head. Brok sat back down on his chair and took a huge gulp out from his mug and wiped his lips with the side of his arm. Kasandra lowered her sword and put it back in its sheath. Jargo remained steadfast and followed the ogre's movements with his wand.

Brok faced the wizard and pointed.

'I think you can put that away. It is of no use here.'

Jargo frowned.

'No use? I think I know several uses for it.'

The barman wiped out a mug from behind the bar with a dirty rag. He put the mug down heavily on the dusty wooden counter and cleared his throat. Everyone looked at the barman intently. He stared back at them, and pointed behind him to a sign:

All magic is forbidden within these walls,
As per Kingdom Rule One Zero Three.

Clannk read the sign out loud. He scratched his head profusely.

'One Zero Three?' he said, confused.

'Oh, damn,' Jargo said, and slumped back down in his chair.

Kasandra started growing bigger in size. It was a sure sign she was not happy. The barman put another drink in front of her and suggested she drink some more to calm her nerves. She took a sip before she spoke.

'So what is this One Zero Three law?'

Jargo put his wand away and folded his hands behind his head. He sat rocking slightly on his creaking chair.

'In short, the law protects only a few places around the kingdom, which ensures that everyone has a haven to retreat to should they need it.'

'So, wizard! Your magic is useless here. And it is where I dominate!' Brok flexed his biceps at Jargo. It bulged like a melon caught between two trees. His arm was enormous compared to anyone else's. Clannk peered with one eye over his drink. He did not seem very impressed. Kasandra stood up onto the dirty bar and slammed her sword into it. She grabbed the handle and rested her chin down on it.

'Brok, you have seen many come through these doors,' said Kasandra cheerfully.

She fluttered her eyes at the ogre, but it did not distract him.

'Yeah, so what about it?' questioned Brok.

'Well, I was wondering if you've happened to see anyone who might interest us.'

'No.'

He took another gulp from his spit brew. Clannk stood up and finished the last of his beer. He wiped foam from his mouth and burped towards the ogre.

Brok stood up and downed his drink, then belched so loudly that it shook a few tables in the bar. The ogre in the corner lifted his sleepy head and looked out from one eye. He then rested his head back down in his arms and continued to sleep.

'Is that all you've got, troll?'

Clannk stood up against the ogre. Being a troll, he was naturally bigger than a human, but he was nowhere near the size of the ogre.

'We are looking for something. Maybe you know where it is.'

'Well, you have come to the right person.'

Brok patted the troll's shoulder heavily.

'But of course, any information comes at a price.'

Kasandra turned and questioned Jargo with her eyes. He shrugged his shoulders and turned his pockets inside out to reveal he had nothing in them.

'What price do you have in mind?' asked the faery.

'How about 1 000 gold pieces?'

Kasandra shuffled around, searching in every bit of clothing that could possibly hide some coins. She remembered she had a gold coin stuck down her sheath and turned it upside down. The sheath shook vigorously as she held it with both arms. A gleaming gold coin fell onto the counter and spun. Everyone at the bar watched it turn until it eventually came to a halt.

'Heads!' Kasandra shouted.

She turned to Brok with her hand held up, expecting a high five. But he just shook his head in disapproval. She picked up the gold coin and held it for inspection.

'Well, here is one. How much information will this get us?'

'One word,' the ogre said bluntly.

The wizard moved towards the bar and leant against it with his elbow firmly tucked into the edge. He folded his hands and smiled.

'Okay, how much information would you give us if I could turn that coin over there into 10 coins?'

Brok stood up immediately and knocked the chair he sat on with his leg.

'Impossible! No magic is allowed here.'

Jargo stood up and pointed his finger into his chest. He drew an X across it and looked up at him.

'Ah, this is where you are wrong. There is magic everywhere. All you have to do is believe.'

The barman whispered into Kasandra's ear.

'Are you sure he hasn't had one too many to drink?'

She smiled back at the barman and nodded her head in approval.

'Kasandra. The coin, if you will.'

He opened his hand so she could give him the coin.

Jargo held the coin up between two fingers. The coin reflected some light as he turned it over in his hand.

Brok stiffened his stance and crossed his arms defensively.

'And how do you propose you will make that coin into 10?'

Jargo bit into the coin and offered it to the ogre. He grabbed it and examined it.

'Okay, so it is a real coin. Now what?'

'Here is the deal. If I can find 10 coins on you, you will give us the information we require,' he said sternly.

'I will save you some hassle, wizard. I do not have any coins on me. I have not been paid yet. So don't bother.'

Brok picked up his chair and slammed it back down. He sat down with his arms folded.

'Agreed. However, let me put this coin away into my pocket over here.'

Jargo held the coin in the palm of his hand and pointed

with his finger. He closed his hand and moved to put the coin back into his pocket.

Kasandra shot up and shouted.

'Hey, that was my coin!'

Jargo put his finger to his lips and summoned her to keep quiet.

'Right. Now, with the coin safely in my pocket, and you, ogre, having no coins on you, how is it possible that you have one stuck behind your ear?'

Brok tried to turn to see if he could see anything behind his ear, but kept on turning in circles. He grabbed both ears and pulled them. He had a very confused look on his face as he frowned.

'There is nothing there, wizard!'

'Oh, isn't there, now?' questioned Jargo.

He jumped up and grabbed the ogre's ear, pulling a coin out from it.

'Then why are you hiding a coin in it?'

Everyone in the room sat up in their chairs and stared with their mouths open at the wizard.

'*Impossible*! I just checked there!'

'Nothing is impossible if you believe,' the wizard said with a smug smile on his face.

'Coin number one.' He put it in his pocket.

Before Brok could move, Jargo began pulling coins from everywhere. From the ear he went to Brok's shirt, then to both of his pants pockets. He produced coins from his mug, and even one straight from his mouth.

Brok stood up again and walked back slowly until he bounced off the wall of the bar.

He waved his hands at the wizard, motioning him to stop.

'What seems to be the matter Ogre? I have only nine coins. I need one more.'

Brok felt himself all over, making sure there was no more to be found.

'There won't be anymore!'

'Then what is that in your shoe?'

Jargo pointed towards the ogre's boot. The boots sat just above his ankles. They were laced all the way to the top. Brok looked down at them and started to untie the right one immediately.

'But all I can feel is my foot,' he said in disbelief.

He pulled the shoe off and examined the inside with his huge hand. He could fit many fingers inside as he tried to feel all sides.

'If I may, ogre. I think I see a coin in there.'

Jargo grabbed the shoe from Brok's hand, and shoved his into it. He felt around staring up at the roof. A surprise lit up his face as he produced yet another coin from Brok's shoe. He tossed the shoe back at the ogre and placed the last coin back into this pocket.

'I do believe that makes 10 coins.'

The wizard sat back down at the table with his beer.

Clannk parked himself next to the wizard. The faery fluttered towards the table and sat with her legs hanging over the edge. The three of them watched patiently as the ogre tried to lace up his shoe. Brok raised his hand up above his head, surrendering himself to them.

'Okay, you win! Ask me what you want and get out of this place!'

Jargo sat up in his chair, put his hands together and tapped his fingers.

'We seek a particular item. And we are hoping you might be aware of any items that might have changed hands here recently.'

Brok angled his head towards the barman and shook it. The barman knelt down behind the bar and pulled out a worn brown sack. It had a very coarse rope tied through it. The barman handed the ogre the sack and wiped his hands on a cloth.

Brok opened up the sack slightly and immediately a light shone from it so brightly that everyone squinted. He closed it up again.

'You might be searching for this.'

Jargo walked over and examined the sack very carefully. He nodded back towards the others at the table. He took the sack and threw it over his shoulder.

'I appreciate your cooperation in this regard.'

'Just take it. It has already caused me problems. I mean, the one and only place I felt safe is now destroyed, thanks to that thing!'

'I am happy to dispose of this, if you would like,' the wizard mentioned.

Brok put his head in his hands and he squeezed his forehead. He nodded his agreement and waved his hand for the bag to go.

Kasandra took flight and flew near the ogre.

'How did you acquire this item?'

The ogre shook his head once more and looked up.

'A bunch of crazy goblins came in singing in rhymes early this morning. They said they had something that was worth more than all the gold in the world. They offered to trade it for some. They always seemed to be laughing. I can remember them chanting about something having to feed their greed. I have collected so much gold over the years that I felt it might be worth the trade. I never felt, for once, that my sense of security would be the sacrifice.'

'Security?' asked Kasandra, puzzled.

'I always felt safe here. I felt untouchable, and now this item brings the bunch of you in here, to play tricks on me!'

Jargo came and put his hand on the ogre's shoulder.

'Don't worry. I think this might be the last time you will see me here.'

'And I will always be your drinking friend,' said Kasandra gleefully.

'Barman, a round of drinks for everyone!' Kasandra shouted.

The rest of the bar cheered in delight.

Outside, in the distance, a noise was heard. It sounded like a heavy fluttering. Clannk stared out the window. All he could see was that wind had started to swing through the trees. He looked up towards the skies and noticed something flying towards the house.

'Um, I see the others coming,' he mumbled.

For a brief moment, there was silence, then a huge thud. The door to the bar creaked opened slowly. For a moment, it seemed that no one would enter. A voice broke the confusion.

'Oh my. I think I need a drink!'

Everyone stared towards the door and noticed a gnome holding the door open. His face was pale and he looked as if he was about to lose his lunch. Another head peered around the door. A dragon's head, sharp with horns.

'You will *not* believe what we just saw!'

Clannk scratched his head and asked, 'What did you see?'

'Well, I can't explain. You will just have to follow me. I think this is what we are looking for.'

Grumblestumps put his hand up and summoned the barman.

'If you'd be so kind as to pour me one of your stiffest drinks?'

Dekrin grabbed the gnome by his collar and picked him up.

'Sorry, Grumblestumps. There is no time. I mean, you saw how fast it travelled.'

'Oh dear.'

'If you could follow me, it is not very far from here,' Dekrin said excitedly.

Kasandra kissed Brok on the cheek and waved goodbye to the barman. They all got up and walked out the door, shutting it tightly behind them. All of them waited with bated breath for the next instruction from the dragon. Dekrin crossed his arms and stared back at them.

'Well? What are you waiting for?'

Chapter 9

The Enslanted Forest of Rottingwood

If you ever found yourself in the Arboretum Labyrinth, you would almost certainly be lost.

The mossy forest floors, with their criss-crossed pathways, covered most of the kingdom's centre. Everything else developed around the outskirts. The forest gave life to flowing rivers, unusual animals and rare plants. It was simply magnificent in its own right, and so complex that it even had maps at each of its divisions – the Woodland, the Plantation, and the Dark Forest. These areas were named so that any traveller would know which part of the forest he or she was lost in. But it was not all gloom inside the landscaped forest. Plenty of pathways were clearly marked; if you made enough effort to travel on these, you would often get to the other side.

The overgrown trees hung lazily in the skies. They stood tall, brushing the clouds as the wind pushed through their tops. It was at moments like this that you could hear the whispering treetops having the last word.

Most travellers took the paths most frequently walked. But some paths appeared untouched. Only the brave ever wandered down these winding death-traps. It was said that once you engaged with these crooked paths, your feet would never let you return. Some said you would only be lost; others thought your life would be lost. Mysterious things happened in the forest.

It started to rain once again throughout the forest. The drops fell down, smacking the ground as they met it. A day of rain had always greeted the area with much anticipation and mud. But the ground did not care. It was happy to move from place to place, even to swim in the river that flowed by. It often rained for short periods, only to be followed by a glorious rainbow shining itself from one side of the forest to the other.

The sounds of galloping feet echoed off the beaten pathway that ran through the forest.

'Hee yah!' shouted a being as it cracked the rein.

In the distance between the clouds, a dragon flew. It soared through the air, with intent.

'Look to your left!' Dekrin shouted.

The others sat stiffly on his back and hung on for dear life.

Jargo looked to his left and saw a clearing between the trees.

'What? Where?' he shouted back.

'Down there! If you look into the clearing you will see it.'

They all leaned carefully to the left to get a better view.

This upset Dekrin's balance, and caused him to spin into a spiral.

'Waaaooohh!' they all shouted.

Kasandra was sure she felt a little bit of her breakfast make its way into her mouth.

Grumblestumps was still tightly fastened to one of the dragon's horns. He sat there with his eyes closed.

Nobody but Clannk was enjoying the breeze flowing across their faces. He enjoyed it so much that he sat at the back with a huge smile on his face while licking the air with his tongue. He patted Kasandra, who sat in front of him. She turned around and looked up at him.

'You are enjoying this a little too much!' she shouted and covered her mouth.

Jargo held onto his hat with his right hand, while the others held tightly onto a rope tied around the dragon's belly.

'We do not see anything!' Jargo shouted towards Dekrin.

'I do not see anything either,' Grumblestumps added, keeping his eyes shut tightly.

Dekrin flapped his wings hard and soared up through a cloud. They all felt some condensation on their faces, but not enough to wet them entirely. He swooped back down towards the opening.

'Hang on tight! We are about to go in!'

Everyone held on to whatever they could get their hands on. Only Clannk sat with his eyes open. Tears of enjoyment ran down the sides of his face from the force of the wind.

Another crack of a rein echoed through the forest. Hooves continued to beat down on the path. Around a corner the unicorn was seen pulling a dark-brown carriage. A twin trail of smoke brought up the rear.

The carriage was enormous, able to hold at least 10 good-sized men. Or two average ogres. It had a door on either side that opened with a rather large, round door knob, and a huge lit torch on each of its corners. A huge wheel, connected to a huge crank, held the carriage up from the ground. The wheel sat perfectly in the centre of the carriage. Right in front sat a very small goblin who wore nothing but a waistcoat and ragged pants. His teeth were crooked, yet a smile always beamed from him.

The unicorn was black with a silver horn. It had adapted its colour over the years as the sun could never find its way into the forest. The darkness of its skin allowed any sun to be absorbed quickly. This warmed up the beast, allowing it to travel long distances. But sunlight was not what gave it its power. Rainbows did – the life's work of each unicorn was to chase down and devour as many rainbows as possible. This ensured their longevity, and made them race from one side of the forest to the other. The goblin had managed, over the years, to con the unicorn into partnering up with him by offering a transportation service inside the forest. At a price, of course. Unicorns do not come cheap.

Dekrin swooped towards the forest floor. His wings flapped heavily as he gained speed. Everyone still hung on for their lives, except for Clannk, who leaned back with his arms stretched out.

'This is fun!' he shouted.

The dragon pointed with his arm to a clearing in the distance.

'There it is again!'

'I see it now. What is that?' questioned Jargo.

'Let me get ahead of it so I can stop it in its tracks. Hang on everyone! The thing is travelling fast.'

Dekrin tucked his head in, and flew as if his life was at stake.

The goblin sat merrily at the front of the carriage, guiding the unicorn down the pathway.

'Don't worry Spike. I see the rainbow you like. We will be there soon, before the high moon.'

The unicorn neighed in approval. It started to gallop with longer strides. Dust flew from behind as it picked up speed. The trails of smoke streaked out in grey lines. The carriage started to rattle as the wheel turned viciously. The goblin noticed a dark object above him. He looked up and saw a leathery belly. His eyes blinked twice.

The dragon flew past and turned around, spreading its wings high across the sky. The unicorn slammed on the brakes in fright. The goblin flew off the carriage and onto the back of the unicorn. One of his hands got caught between the reins, which flung him upside down. The unicorn came to a standstill and snorted. Cool air escaped from its nostrils. The dragon lowered itself onto the ground and sat down. Jargo slapped the dragons back. Grumblestumps still held tightly onto the rope he had fastened to Dekrin. His eyes were covered by his hand.

'Is it over yet?' he ventured.

Kasandra slid off the dragon's back and fluttered onto the floor. She looked around.

'I think I am going to be sick,' she moaned.

Clannk climbed off and stretched his gangly body. He placed his arms at his sides and yawned.

'This flying has made me sleepy,' he said.

Jargo pulled out his spiral wand and waved it at the goblin. With a flick of his hand, he untied the goblin from the reins. The goblin fell straight to the ground, then picked himself up and wiped the mud from his face. The goblin bowed to those who were watching his every move.

'I mean no harm, I will convince you with my charm,' he sang.

Kasandra grabbed her sword from its sheath. She flew up to the goblin and stared into his eyes.

'You look like one of *them*. Now where is it?' she snarled.

She held her sword up against the goblin's chest. He looked down at it nervously, and surrendered with his arms above his head.

'I do not know what you look for, understand this for sure.'

'You would stop talking in rhymes, goblin, if you knew what was good for you.'

Her sword tip started to creep up the goblin's nose.

'I am not aware of what you require, for I am not a liar.'

Kasandra growled at the goblin. She became increasingly angry. It was never a good sign, especially for those were not aware of her capabilities. It had always been a mystery why Silvercrown faeries were the only faery kind to be able to grow in stature. It was said it was due to all the anger growing inside them that had to find its way out. But it was indeed the anger that made them grow bigger. The anger could never be spurred by themselves but by those who created it by a word or an action. Kasandra was the only one who got a kick out of becoming bigger than she really was. It made her feel like she could stand up to just about anyone who had dared cross her path.

'ENOUGH of this rhyming!'

The goblin broke out into a sweat.

'Please do not hurt me. I am not really a goblin.'

'Well, you sure look like one. Do you bleed like one?'

'No! Please do not hurt me. As you can see I am very

far away from Goblin City. I chose many years ago not to serve Glasshook anymore.'

Jargo looked down at Grumblestumps who still covered his eyes with his hands. Jargo grabbed his arm and lowered it. He noticed that Grumblestumps' eyes were still closed.

'Grumble, I think it's safe to open your eyes now.'

Grumblestumps blinked his eyes a few times. He realised he did not have his reading, writing and arithmetic glasses on. He pulled them from his shirt pocket and put them back on.

'Oh, back on solid ground. Good,' he said, shaking.

Kasandra grabbed the goblin's waistcoat and pulled it towards her.

'So how are we to believe you do not serve Glasshook anymore?'

The goblin stood with his arms still above his head and cleared his throat.

'If you release me from your sturdy grip, I would be honoured to demonstrate my non-allegiance.'

Kasandra let go of his waistcoat, but held her sword close to his chest.

'If I may I will show you now.'

The goblin slowly took off his waistcoat and turned around. On his back stood a word tattooed.

'Banished, GH.'

Clannk scratched his head with his crooked finger.

'B-A-N-I-S...' he struggled.

Kasandra glared at Clannk and motioned him to stop.

'Banished? Why were you banished, goblin?'

'Well, we are all for gold and greed. And after years of serving under him, I became tired of him.'

Jargo stood with his arms folded, his wand sticking out slightly between them. The goblin continued.

'So I slowly started acquiring less gold for Glasshook

while I grew my own greed. I managed to steal about a third of his wealth over the years, and no one was the wiser until one day.'

'So what happened on this day?' asked Kasandra.

'It was a silly error on my part, but someone accidentally fell through my secret hideout. Over the years, the door, which apparently led to nowhere inside Goblin City, was always ignored. The story in the city was always told that there was nothing of interest behind it. So in my brilliance, I decided to exploit it. But over time the door became brittle from the sun's rays beating down on it. And through a mindless brawl one day for the amusement of Glasshook, several goblins flung themselves at the door for fun. The door broke into pieces and there I stood, holding a bag full of gold, staring back at everyone looking in.'

Kasandra smiled and lowered her sword to the ground.

'I guess they caught you gold-handed,' she smirked.

'And red-faced,' the goblin replied.

The goblin put his waistcoat back on and fastened it with the only wooden button stitched in place.

'So I was banished for life from Goblin City and have the mark to prove it.'

Jargo stepped forward and pulled Kasandra aside. He put his hands on her shoulders and gestured with a nod of his head. She slid her sword back into its sheath and adjusted her helmet on her head.

'So, goblin, how did you manage to acquire such a magnificent beast? Not to mention the carriage,' she asked.

The goblin beamed with his crooked teeth. He walked up to the unicorn and rubbed its belly. The beast lowered its head and nudged the goblin with its nose, which caused the goblin to fly onto the ground.

'Ha ha. Yes, Spike. I do owe you a treat. Let's get you something to eat.' He grabbed a satchel from the carriage and opened it up. There was something gold and shiny inside. He grabbed a handful and offered it to the unicorn to eat. With one big mouthful, the unicorn devoured all he had in his hands.

Clannk walked over excitedly.

'You have something to eat. I need a treat too.'

Grumblestumps walked over to the goblin and asked to look inside the satchel. He was very inquisitive to know what this unicorn was so interested in eating. Grumblestumps pulled out a handful of the gold stuff. He examined it intently.

'I do not believe this!' he exclaimed.

'What is it Grumblestumps?' asked Dekrin.

'I thought these were but a myth, but here I stand with a handful of it.'

'It looks like gold flowers.' Dekrin added.

'This is no ordinary flower. This is a Golden Clover. The rarest of rare finds, I might add.'

Grumblestumps put the golden clovers back into the satchel.

'How did you acquire so much of the golden clover?'

The goblin pointed at the unicorn and smiled.

'All thanks to my trusty steed.'

Dekrin sauntered over to the unicorn and looked it up and down.

'So how does this horse with a horn find these flowers?' asked the dragon.

'This is no ordinary horse. This is a unicorn. In these parts of the kingdom it is known as a Rainbow Chaser. Their sole aim in life is to consume as many rainbows as possible to ensure longevity. The interesting thing is at the end of every rainbow, the golden clovers grow. They start out as ordinary green clovers, but the magic power of the rainbow turns them into golden ones. These clovers hold smaller amounts of the rainbow's powers. This is why I can only give a few at a time to the unicorn. It allows the unicorn to power his way to the next rainbow. In these forests, rainbows are common, but finding the end of the rainbow is a challenge. You have to be extremely quick.'

Kasandra flew up to the unicorn and felt its horn.

'Sharp.'

'Piercing, to be exact. I wouldn't suggest anyone gets in its way,' the goblin explained.

The faery landed back down next to the goblin and put her arm around his shoulders.

'So who gets to ride in your carriage?'

'Anyone may ride in my carriage. For a fee, of course.'

'And has anyone taken a paid ride in the last few days?'

'There was a gentleman a little while ago who asked to get to the edge of the Dark Forest.'

Jargo's eyes lit up at the sound of the word. He stepped forward.

'Why would he ask to go to the Dark Forest? Everyone knows how dangerous it can be in there.'

'I understand, wizard, but I do not turn down gold. Especially the kind he offered to me.'

Kasandra looked puzzled.

'And what kind would that be?' she asked.

'A lot of it,' the goblin replied.

Jargo knew no one ever deliberately needed to go to the Dark Forest, let alone wanted to go. It concerned him, since the last time he ventured into the Dark Forest things happened which he never wanted to repeat. Losing his favourite coat was one thing, but he certainly did not want to lose another.

'Can you take us to where you dropped this man off?'

'I certainly can, for a price of course.'

The goblin smiled and held out his hand.

In a blink of an eye, Kasandra pulled out her broad edged sword and held it up against the goblin's throat. She grabbed his hand with hers and squeezed it tightly.

'Is this enough for the fare?' she enquired.

The goblin swallowed hard and nodded.

'Good. If you do not mind, I will ride up in front with you. The rest can ride in the back.'

Dekrin looked at the carriage carefully. He knew he would never fit into it and offered to fly alongside the carriage. The others eagerly opened up the doors to the carriage and scrambled in to get the best seat. Clannk fiddled with everything inside, keen to know what it could do.

'Would you not touch everything?' moaned Grumblestumps.

Clannk folded his hands quickly and stared out through the open window on the door.

'Brace yourself everyone. This is going to go quickly,' shouted the goblin.

'Spike, find the rainbow if you like.'

The unicorn reared up onto his back legs and neighed triumphantly. Within a second, it pulled off with great speed. The carriage rocked back and forth as it gained momentum. Those who were inside the carriage bounced around in their seats as they hung onto whatever they could get their hands on. Once the unicorn picked up speed, the carriage found its rhythm. The unicorn followed a mossy path filled with debris from the earlier rain. Leaves scattered around the forest floor were scooped up into the air as the unicorn galloped by. The path wound through the trees. Wildlife and Wallow-shriek Birds meandered through the shrubs.

Everything whisked by in a blur as the unicorn galloped as fast as it could go.

A shadowy figure walked silently and stopped at a sign:

Dark Forest – tread carefully or these steps may be your last.

The figure smiled and twirled his moustache. He tipped his cavalier hat and took a short bow.

'I shall tread carefully, zen.'

The Dark Forest was constantly surrounded by an eerie mist. It lay low over the pathways, and the deeper you travelled, the denser it became. Night creatures dwelled within the corners, lying in wait for victims. Danger lurked behind every tree, and followed you as you walked by. The occasional howl of an animal echoed through the darkness. The figure pushed some shrubbery aside and stepped over it. His leather boots continued on. They reached his shins, and his pants were tucked neatly into them.

Dekrin flapped alongside the carriage. He looked up ahead to where the path was meandering, noticing the mist that had started to gather in the distance. A few birds circled low above the mist. They screeched at each other as if they were passing a message along. One caught sight of what was coming in their direction. It suddenly flew up and hid in the nearest tree. The others quickly followed; they sat still, in a row. The carriage came screaming by. The mist lifted for them as they ran through. The eyes of the birds followed the carriage until it disappeared down the path.

'How much further, goblin?' shouted Kasandra.

'Oh, not much now. See up ahead? The forest is turning from brown to black. The entrance to the Dark Forest is there.'

Kasandra took her sword and banged it on the roof of the carriage. She turned and leant towards the window of the door.

'We are almost there. I suggest you hold onto your hats! I think we are about to have a sudden stop!'

Jargo looked at Grumblestumps grabbing the nearest handle tightly. He grabbed his hat again and held his other hand up against the roof. Clannk stuck his head out through the window. A hedge ran along the path, separated by a gap. A sign saying Dark Forest was entwined with a creeper's tendrils. The unicorn slammed on brakes and skidded on the wet moss path. The carriage wobbled awkwardly, then jack-knifed, coming to a halt right next to the beast. Clannk was still hanging out of the window. He stretched out and patted the unicorn on its neck. The faery glared at the goblin and stood up.

'What the heck was that?'

'My dear faery friend, that was the end of your carriage ride.'

'You have to be kidding!' she exclaimed.

'I appreciate your patronage, and please watch your step when vacating.'

'If you don't shut up, my sword will be vacating its sheath for your chest.'

The other door of the carriage swung open and the wizard climbed out. Grumblestumps stood at the edge of the door, looking shaky. Jargo extended his hand and helped the gnome down to the ground.

'I think I need to find safer and slower alternatives for travelling around,' Grumble suggested.

The unicorn snorted and kicked the ground impatiently. The goblin pulled back on the reins tightly.

'Spike, if you like, we may vacate just after I say goodbye to my mate.'

Clannk still hung through the window of the carriage. He tried to pull himself free but found climbing out was not as easy as climbing in. Jargo saw the troll struggling and pulled out his spiral wand. He mumbled something into his beard and flicked his wand. Clannk suddenly became free and landed back onto his feet.

'I appreciate you assistance, goblin. One last question: did you see if this person was carrying anything unusual with him?' Jargo asked.

The goblin scratched his chin and thought for a moment.

'The only thing I remember was the blinding light that occasionally came out the carriage while we were on our way. I thought it might be the sun trying to get through the darkness of the trees, but it had been raining then.'

'This might be someone we are looking for. Did the light look much like this?'

Jargo asked Clannk to give him the bag which he had flung over his shoulder. The troll handed over the bag and stood back. The wizard opened the bag slightly and a blinding light beamed out from it. A sound emenated from the beam as it tried to escape the darkness. Jargo quickly tied the bag up tightly. The goblin stood and stared with his mouth wide open.

'The light... the light is the most magnificent thing I have seen! It shone brighter than gold on a hot summer's day.'

'The light is indeed blinding and should be treated with the utmost caution,' Jargo replied.

The goblin smiled with his crooked teeth and pointed to the Dark Forest sign. Kasandra walked up to the sign and read it carefully.

'I am sure we will be just fine in here. Right, Jargo?'

The wizard just looked at her and scratched his beard.

Kasandra noticed some muddy footprints near the sign. She knelt down and ran her fingers over the print. It looked like a reasonably sized foot.

'These prints look fresh. I am sure we will catch up with this individual sooner rather than later.'

Clannk walked over to the faery and put his hands on his hips, looking down.

'These not troll. I know troll.'

'You are right. This is human. But for some reason I have never seen this type much around the kingdom.'

The unicorn snorted impatiently and scraped the ground with its hooves. The goblin climbed back onto the carriage and grabbed the reins.

'I shall wish you a safe journey ahead, as it is time for my Steed to be fed!'

The goblin cracked the reins and the unicorn sped off, kicking mud high into the air. The dragon watched them drive off into the misty forest.

Kasandra pushed her helmet up and fluttered her wings.

'We have no time to waste, let us get going.'

'Would you like to take the lead?' Jargo asked.

'Yes, I think I have this one, thanks!' she replied.

Kasandra flew into the Dark Forest first, followed by Jargo. He pulled his black wand from its velvet pouch and followed the faery. Clannk followed, clumsily pushing over some shrubs as he walked. The dragon brought up the rear and looked around to familiarise himself with his strange new surroundings.

The forest creaked and cracked as the wind swept through it. The shadows walked awkwardly to and fro from the edges of the trees. A damp, stale smell hung over the forest, eagerly awaiting nostrils to irritate. Several cobwebs lay scattered in between the bent branches. Small creatures scurried across the forest floor and hid among holes in the trees. A few larger birds flapped their wings, trying to settle in the cool high above the ground. The trees grew higher and wider the further the paths drew into the forest. Footsteps clopped onto the cobbled pathway, which forced itself into a clearing. The clearing had an incredibly large tree growing in the centre. The tree had a huge hole at the base. Its branches stretched high into the skies. It stood bare, looking almost dead. Many dried-up pieces of bark and branches lay scattered around. A few rocks lay like a staircase up towards the top of the tree. The tree looked like it had been standing there for centuries. It stood motionless, defying any effort nature made to stir it. A figure stood still at the edge of the cobbled pathway and looked towards the eerie tree.

'Mmm, zis must be it.'

He twirled his moustache and smiled. He held his other arm behind him, with a hand tucked into the back of his pants. He looked up towards the top of the huge tree and back down. The sun tried to make its way through the dark clouds, which moved high above. The figure covered his face slightly from the glare.

The wind picked up slightly and gushed its way through the path. The faery flew slightly above the path they were following, watching the muddy footprints that lead in their direction.

'Jargo, do you know why this human would want to spend time here in the Dark Forest?'

Jargo stopped for a moment, then carried on after Kasandra.

'I can only assume that it wants to reach the Tree of Acknowledgment,' he said.

'What is Ack ...ack ...?' Clannk said, puzzled.

Grumblestumps walked up next to the troll to explain.

'Acknowledgement is a declaration or avowal of one's own act, to give it legal validity.'

Clannk frowned with a blank expression on his face. Jargo smiled at Grumblestumps.

'I think with regards to the tree, the definition is applied differently.'

'And how is it defined in the kingdom?' Grumblestumps asked.

'The Tree of Acknowledgement is unique. It possesses a power that many seek. However, it only relinquishes the power to those who truthfully seek it.'

The warriors all paused in their tracks.

'I think we should understand what we are getting ourselves into before we head into the direction of this tree,' Kasandra replied.

Jargo nodded in agreement.

'If I may continue, the Tree of Acknowledgement has given everything in the Enslanted Forests of Rottingwood life and meaning. However, the forest was always honest in its approach to life. It was once said that a passerby collapsed near the tree one day, almost at his final breath. His last words were his wish to live, as he did not want to leave his loved ones behind to bear the sorrow of his death. As he lay there, he felt an energy picking him up off the ground, carrying him to his loved ones. He envisioned himself in the arms of his loved ones as he passed away. The tree gave life in an unselfish act, even if it was the last moment this man could experience.'

Grumblestumps gestured with his hand in the air.

'May I elaborate for clarity?

'You may do so,' replied Jargo.

'The tree would only grant a wish, if you will, to one who truly wanted it from the heart?'

'Yes, indirectly. However, you cannot ask it for material things. Which some have found out the hard way.'

'And do you think this human is on his way to have his wish fulfilled?' Kasandra asked.

'I am sure we will find out soon enough.'

Jargo waved his hand and walked on. The rest followed closely. The cobbled pathway was nearing a clearing, with a tall tree standing high above the rest.

The figure stood a few metres from the tree. He drew his fencing sword from his side. He looked up and down the blade, rubbing it with his gloved hand.

The musketeer pointed the sword at the tree with meaning.

'Aah, we meet for ze first time, tree. You shall give me what I seek.'

His eyes stared straight at the tree, never leaving its dark, barky body.

'What iz zis? No answer? You shall answer me!'

He heard footsteps behind him. Without turning, he smiled in the delight of the noise.

'Vizitors, aah! I like Vizitors!'

At the edge of the clearing, Kasandra and the rest stood still. They noticed a man who wore a cavalier hat, brown leather boots and a frilly white shirt tucked into a rather tight pair of brown cotton pants. They all noticed that he had his gloved left hand tucked neatly behind him in his pants.

'Good day, traveller. What do you seek in these parts?' asked Jargo.

The figure turned around with a twirl on one foot. He landed perfectly and bowed towards them. They all walked up slowly to get a better look at him. He stood twirling his moustache once again.

'Aah, yes. A traveller indeed. And a group of you to investigate reasonz why I am here.'

Kasandra noticed a satchel around his shoulders, containing a small, round bulge.

'Excuse me, but it is not you we seek, but rather what you might have.'

The musketeer pulled his nose up at the faery.

'What iz zis? A little runt of a woman? She does not speak to me until spoken to.'

Kasandra turned and looked at the rest with her mouth open. Dekrin frowned as he looked on.

'Dear Sir, I am Jargo, post-wizard for the kingdom. We do not mean you any harm. We are on a quest to help retrieve the kingdom's stolen marbles.'

'Aah, Wizard. I am Zacuree. And those who dare to speak when spoken to, can call me Zac! Mighty Musketeer from Zampheer.'

Derkin laughed out loud and pushed the troll. They both looked at each other and snickered.

'Why do you find zis funny, Dragon?' Zachuree asked.

'I do not think you can claim mightiness in the kingdom. Besides, look at the size of you; what harm could you do?'

The musketeer walked up to them and stared into each one's eyes.

'You zee? Zese eyes fear NO ONE!'

Kasandra stood shaking her head. Her helmet rocked back and forth. The musketeer turned and looked at her.

'Look at zis. She does not even fit into zis helmet. How in zis kingdom could she possibly put fear into zis man?'

Clannk looked confused as usual.

'Um, what man?' he asked.

'Z-A-C-U-R-E-E! Zis is me! You imbecile!'

Jargo stepped foward.

'Excuse me, Zac. But what accent is this? I am not familiar with it in our kingdom?'

The musketeer smiled once again and rubbed his moustache.

'I am from a faraway land called Zampheer. We speak ze language of love and know no fear. I am ze French Musketeer!'

Everyone looked at each other and burst out laughing.

'Zis is not funny!'

Zacuree grabbed his sword from his side and pointed it menacingly at them.

'How dare you insult me! For zis I will duel with your best fighter!'

Jargo looked at Dekrin, and the dragon stared out into the sky. Kasandra pulled her sword to meet his. But the musketeer slammed her sword away from his.

'You have to be kidding! I do not want to fight zis puny runt!'

Grumblestumps pulled at Jargo's robe and pointed at the faery.

'Excuse me again, Zac. But you do not want to get this puny runt of a faery angry!' he snickered.

The rest of the warriors giggled under their breaths. Except for the faery.

Kasandra pushed her helmet above her eyes, and glared back at the musketeer.

'I dare you to duel with me, musketeer!'

'I do not waste my time, for I am undefeated and only battle zose who are worth duelling.'

'Is this so? I think you will be surprised! Now duel me!' she shouted.

'I shall say zis only once, Runt! I will not duel you!'

He took his glove off his hand and folded in half. He

held it for a moment, then swung it, hitting the faery in the face. He turned away and walked, tucking his sword back onto his side.

Kasandra stood motionless. Slowly but surely, she started to grow.

'I think you just made me mad. Everyone, step back. This is going to get ugly!'

The dragon took a few steps back and sat down. Clannk made sure he found a rock to lean up against. Jargo stood still with his arms folded. Grumblestumps grabbed a cloth from his pouch to clean his glasses. He was making sure he would not miss out on the fun. The musketeer stood with his back to Kasandra, unaware of her change in size.

He spoke.

'If you must know, a duel is acknowledged by a glove slap. So, if you wish to duel, I suggest you do ze same.'

Kasandra's anger made her grow to human size; she was fuming. She grabbed a piece of bark from the ground and walked up to behind him.

'Is this acceptance enough for you?' she asked.

She raised it above her head and smashed it down on his hat.

The others all shouted in unison and grimaced.

'Waaooohhh! That has got to hurt!'

The musketeer's hat fell to the ground. He stood still, wiping the bark pieces from his hair. Bending down, he picked up his hat and dusted it off. He turned around and to his shock noticed the faery was about his height.

'What iz zis? I do not deal with magic!'

Jargo laughed.

'This is not my doing Zac. You are on your own. I told you not to make her angry!'

Zacuree grabbed his sword from his side. He tucked his left hand into the back of his trousers.

'What name do zay call you?'

'My name is Kasandra. And don't you forget it.'

'Aah, yes. Kassie. Let us see what you have got. I shall make it easy for you. I shall only fight you with one hand.'

'Don't call me Kassie!' she shouted. The faery grew a little more.

The musketeer's eyes lit up with delight as he held out his fencing sword to duel. She met his sword with hers. The sound of the swords echoed through the forest. Kasandra's helmet sat perfectly tight on her head, with her hair scrunched underneath. She lifted herself above the ground with her wings.

'Aah, you like to play dirty.'

Zacuree kicked sand into her face with his boot. It blinded her for a moment and she landed back on the ground.

'I can play dirty too!' he chuckled.

She grabbed the helmet off her head and threw it at him. He swatted the helmet with his sword and caught it on the tip.

'Zis I shall dispose of.'

He flicked her helmet into the bushes. She held her sword tightly and charged him with it. He moved off to the side as she ran by, skidding in her tracks.

'Maybe I shall fight wiz one leg only? No?'

He stood up on one leg, balancing perfectly. It made her even angrier; she raced up again towards him. She held her sword with both hands above her head, ready to drive the blade into his chest. She ran screaming in frustration. Again, he hopped to the side as she continued to pass him. He yawned and closed his eyes.

'Wake me up when you are finished chasing yourself,' he said sarcastically.

The others rolled around on the floor laughing.

Grumblestumps wiped his teary eyes with his sleeve. It was the best entertainment they had seen in a long time.

She stopped in her tracks, puffing and panting.

'I am going to knock your head off!'

'Ok, Kassie. I shall say zis. If you beat me in a duel, you can have anyzing you want, no?'

She thought about his offer for a moment while catching her breath.

'Okay, musketeer. Here is the offer. If I beat you in a duel, you give me what you have in that satchel of yours. I am sure you do not need it?'

'What, zis?'

He opened up the satchel and a blinding light shone from it. They all shut their eyes and urged him to close the bag.

'Yes, I do not know what zis is, but I won it from a very stupid goblin. You may have it; it has no meaning for me.'

For once, Kasandra smiled and raised her sword towards the skies.

'Let's get it on!'

'Get it on we shall.' Zac replied.

They marched up to each other and smashed their swords together. Kasandra held her sword with both her hands as he did with only one. They pushed the swords up against their chests and stared at each other for a brief moment. Kasandra, with a grunt, pushed him away from her as their swords met again. The clashing sounds of their swords meeting sounded like a war song singing out into the forest. They duelled equally well and the musketeer seemed impressed with the faery's strength and tenacity. He had a constant smile on his face, which made the others wonder if he really liked duelling with a larger-than-usual faery. The musketeer walked up and stood on one of the rocks that laddered itself up towards the tree. The higher he climbed, the more Kasandra duelled with him in flight. The sweat started to drip from their brows as the fight wore on. There were tremendous ducks, dives and falls. There was even a moment where they both gave each other time to catch their breath.

'I must admit, warrior. You have zurprized me wiz your stamina. Where did you learn to fight like zis?' he said.

He took a moment to catch his breath. He put his hand on his thighs, breathing heavily. She puffed and blew her messy hair from her face.

'This is not a time to question why, but to do or die! Well, something like that!'

'Zen I shall end zis, once and for all.'

They chased each other around the tree, jumping over rocks, to settle finally on each side of the tree, panting.

'Okay, faery. I shall give you the chance to come around once more, and I shall wait.'

Kasandra took flight and flew around the top of the tree, holding her sword above her head again. She swooped towards the musketeer, who stood suspiciously still. He pressed his back tightly against the tree, his sword down. She felt it was a little too easily but was eager to attack at the chance. She flew in, wanting to drive the sword into his chest and end it once and for all. But for the final time, a slight movement from him to the side was all he needed. Kasandra's sword went straight into the tree as she flew into it. She hung there, still holding onto her sword tightly. She felt him walk up slowly behind her and press his fencing sword into her back. The other warriors all stood up in shock. They could not believe Kasandra was just about defeated. They held their breath.

'Zis is game over, Runt!' he smirked.

He twirled his moustache in satisfaction. At that moment, she knew she had to do something. She felt the pressure of his sword reduce. He was too preoccupied with that silly soup-strainer above his lip.

'No it isn't!' she remarked.

She closed her eyes for a few seconds, and immediately she changed size. Her hands let go of the sword and she dropped to the ground. The musketeer, in desperation, drove his sword, hoping to stab her. But his delay caused him to drive it straight into the tree. The sword wedged itself there. She rolled to the floor and did a backward flip. Halfway into the flip, she grabbed the three daggers from her belt. The musketeer, still holding onto his sword, turned and followed her with his eyes. In one swift movement, she fired the three daggers at the musketeer. One pegged his hand to the tree through his sleeve, another pegged the collar of his shirt, and the last pinned his arm to the tree. She landed back onto the ground, kneeling on one knee, her arm still extended from the throw.

The warriors all jumped in the air and cheered.

'I see you got the point!'

She laughed out loud and wiped her hair from her face.

'Zis is not possible!' he shouted.

Kasandra walked over to the tree and retrieved her sword. She wiped the blade on her pants and held it to the stranded musketeer's neck.

'Time to end this. It was so SLICE to meet you.'

'No no! Take what you want. Spare my life! I shall leave zis place and never come back.'

Kasandra took the satchel from his shoulder and slung it over hers.

'I think I will be keeping this,' she smiled.

Within an instant, the musketeer disappeared into thin air. Kasandra wiped the dust from her face. She could not understand what had just happened.

The warriors came running to her. Grumblestumps hugged her.

'Well done!' they all shouted.

Clannk patted her heavily on the back. Jargo shook his head at Dekrin, who just smiled.

'Could someone just tell me what happened to the musketeer?'

Jargo put his arm around Kasandra and looked down at her.

'The Tree of Acknowledgement just happened! Amazing, since the last disaster we had here left the tree useless.'

'What disaster?' asked Dekrin.

'The Tirade of the Fire Goblins. But that story is for another time. I think I know where we need to go to find those goblins.'

Clannk shuffled restlessly. He rubbed his stomach and felt it growl with hunger.

'Me need to eat soon, or I get mad.'

Dekrin nodded his head in agreement.

Grumblestumps shuffled in his pouch and pulled out a potion. The label read *Pang's Potion*. He handed the vile potion to Clannk to drink.

'This should rid you of your hunger for a few hours. But you are correct, Clannk; we need to set up camp soon and rest. These last few days have been very eventful.'

'Fair enough. Since we are all nicely close together, I think it would be best if you transport us the efficient way.'

Everyone knew they were about to travel with Jargo.

'Places to where I want to be.'

They all disappeared into a puff of dust. The Tree creaked, alone.

Chapter 10

Slush of Kremkin

The shadows moved slowly across the floor of the misty forest. Soon, the rustling of the forest canopy was just a memory, as the five watched the forest give way to bubbling marshes and sulphur-infested slush. They stopped at the edge of the wasteland that lay festering between Ogreville and Goblin City.

'Did someone fart?'

'Then what's that smell? It's even made my nose-hairs fall out.'

'I believe we are officially in the Slush of Kremkin,' said Jargo.

The dragon sniffed the foul air. It tickled his nose and he sneezed.

'Ugh, what *is* this smell?'

Grumblestumps adjusted his pouch around his waist and fixed his hat while he spoke.

'I do believe the smell emanating from this marsh-like

area is sulphur. It is an element that comes in crystalline form in these parts. However, the erratic rain patterns cause the huge crystals to melt and form these marshes or ponds. It slowly bubbles under the high humidity here, and forms vapours with which I am sure your noses have shaken hands.'

Kasandra closed her nose tightly between her fingers. She shook her head in disapproval.

'Well, it stinks! Do we need to be here?'

Jargo found a nearby stump to rest his behind on.

'I brought us here as the Slush of Kremkin fits snugly between Ogreville and Goblin City. I am sure we will cross paths with a goblin or two in here.'

Clannk's stomach rumbled and roared like a hungry animal. Dekrin looked behind him to see if it was a real animal lurking in between the bog. Clannk patted his stomach to keep quiet.

'Just my tummy. Hungry. I have to eat.'

Jargo surveyed the area. They sat between a few dead trees at the edge of a bog. There was a little bit of rainwater gurgling by. The ground underfoot was dry and filled with tiny stones. It felt like a good enough place to set up for the night. The night was light, as the three moons were full. They shone down onto the yellow marshes, casting a yellow light all around.

'This looks like a good place to settle tonight before we head off into this slush in the morning,' Jargo said.

'But what about this smell?' replied Kasandra still pegging her nose with her fingers.

Grumblestumps scrambled in his pouch. He pulled out a few bottles and threw some of each one's contents into a small mortar. He began pounding it with a pestle until was a fine powder. He walked over to the bog nearest to them and filled up one of his empty bottles. He threw the yellow bog water into the mortar and proceeded to stir the mixture into a paste. It slowly turned red and started to smell of strawberries.

'I have made a paste that you need to put on your lips. This will help to mask the sulphurous smell. What you *will* smell is a delightful scent of strawberries.'

Grumblestumps held the mortar for each of them to take a fingerful of the red paste.

They all looked at it intently. Clannk smelt it and smiled.

'Mmm, it smells good, I want to eat it!'

'I would not do that if I were you. It will make you pass gas smelling of sulphur and rotten strawberries.'

Kasandra shuddered and covered her eyes with her hand.

'I don't even want to *think* what that will smell like.'

'Now, if you follow what I do, you will be certain not to smell sulphur for at least a day.'

He scooped the red paste up with his finger and wiped it carefully onto his top and bottom lip. He smacked his lips against each other so the paste would stick properly. The rest followed his instructions carefully. Once they were done, they all smiled back at each other. They noticed that not only were their lips a bright red, but their teeth too. Clannk pointed at the dragon and laughed out loud.

'Look, dragon is a girl!'

The rest looked back at each other and burst out laughing. They laughed so much that Jargo was bent over in hysterics. Kasandra and Grumblestumps rolled around the floor while Dekrin stood leaning up against a tree pointing to the troll with tears rolling down his eyes from laughter. Through the fit of laughter, Kasandra shouted out, 'I smell strawberries! Strawberries!'

The comment caused them to laugh even more, until

they ran out of breath. One by one, they slowly got up from the floor and dusted themselves off. Grumblestumps took out a cloth, wiped his eyes and cleaned his glasses. Jargo cleared his throat and pulled out his wand.

'If I may, it would be festive if we had a fire.'

'I go fetch wood,' Clannk said eagerly.

'No need, troll.'

Jargo waved his spiral wand towards the centre of their campsite.

'Fire is where I want it to be.'

Within seconds a roaring fire sprang up, crackling and popping as the wood burnt brightly. Kasandra walked over to the fire and warmed up her hands. She looked back at Dekrin, who just looked the other way.

'I could do that if I wanted to, I just don't have the need to,' he protested.

'Then why can't you breathe fire, dragon?' she asked.

'It's not that I do not want to, I choose not to.'

Clannk got up and walked off carefully, avoiding stepping into any of the stinking marshes. He balanced uneasily on a rock, bouncing from one to the other to avoid stepping into any slush. They watched him disappear into the night.

Dekrin looked puzzled.

'Where do you think he went?'

'Maybe he needed more than just a rest?' she asked.

A few minutes went by; they heard some footsteps coming closer. Clannk appeared, holding something in both of his hands. He walked up to the others and threw down a bunch of dead birds. Grumblestumps stared at the birds. He was not sure how many there were, but it seemed quite a few.

'How do you eat your bird?' Clannk asked.

'With my hands?' the faery replied.

'No, I mean cooked.'

'Crispy for me,' the dragon said.

They all nodded in agreement. Clannk smiled and grabbed a bird. He proceeded to pluck the feathers off. He climbed a tall tree and snapped off a few branches. He grabbed the birds and shoved the sticks through them, criss-crossing the birds so they all hung nicely above the fire.

'Ready in half an hour,' he said proudly.

They all relaxed against something as comfortable as possible, and shared a few stories about their lives. Kasandra told them a story of how she was at one of her favourite drinking holes when a traveller challenged her to a drinking contest. She beat him by two drinks and watched him collapse to the floor. They announced her to be the victor before she ran outside and threw up into a trough, almost filling it.

Grumblestumps told his story of how he accidently created a potion that could cure warts on your feet, but that turned your hair blue. He discussed for a several minutes the benefits of having blue hair, which seems to keep the bugs at bay. Insects see blue as fire, so they avoid anything blue. So you can safely say you will sleep tight without any bed bugs biting.

Dekrin told a story about when he was just a young dragon and his father brought some Flurt meat back from hunting. They were starving – they hadn't eaten for days – so his father ate too much meat. A piece got stuck in his throat, causing him to choke. Dekrin became frantic and, out of desperation, grabbed a sharp fossilised claw he had found in their cave. He jammed it into his father's foot. His father bellowed in pain, which dislodged the meat in his throat. He then patted Dekrin on the shoulder and carried on eating, with the claw still jammed into his foot.

Jargo told of his first day in the Palace of Elders. It was

a magnificent day to be able to retire to a simplified life. All you had to do was what you felt like. He told them how he loved to tinker with human magic. He explained a trick of pulling a rabbit out of the hat to the other wizards. But for some reason, he lost the rabbit. A few weeks later, he thought he had found it – only to find that it had spawned enough babies to eat all the shrubs in the garden. This was the first time he'd had to stand in front of the council to explain himself. Needless to say, he quickly fixed the garden up with a flick of a wand. The easy life, he called it.

Clannk told his story of how the most enjoyable thing in Aldedde was eating. He became so fascinated by making food to eat that he started to experiment. He started to collect many unusual ingredients. Through trial and error, he developed a very unusual dish he named hollow pie. He explained to them that once you start to eat, it tastes like more. He warned that if you ate too much of it, you could explode. He said one day they fooled one of the trolls into eating too much; he exploded and died. They hid him away for several days. When the senior troll came back to their village, he was not impressed. Another troll took one of Clannk's pies and threw it at the senior troll. It hit him in the face, but he just ate everything and walked away. He said it was worth the time away to be able to receive a pie and eat it all too.

Dekrin smelt the delicious birds cooking and licked his red-pasted lips. Clannk grabbed the birds from the fire and tasted each one. He confirmed them ready and offered each one a bird on a stick. The biggest one he offered to Dekrin. Everyone sat around the fire, munching on their stick birds. The meat tore off easily and melted in their mouths. A mumble of approvals went around, complimenting the cook on a good job. When they were all finished, they lay down, looking up at the three moons.

'Burp!'

Kasandra wiped her mouth and apologised.

'Burrp!' Jargo smiled and picked his teeth.

'Burrrp! Excuse me,' said Grumblestumps.

Clannk and Dekrin burped together. It was Dekrin who extended the burp. They all looked up as he burped towards the sky. A few sparks flew from his mouth. In shock, he closed it quickly. He held his hand out; it was shaking.

'What was that?'

'It looked like sparks!' Kasandra screamed in delight.

'You almost created fire, it seems,' Grumblestumps added.

Dekrin stood up and walked from side to side. He looked baffled.

'But how? I did not do anything. I did not even think about wanting to do it.'

Grumblestumps walked up to the dragon and laid his hand on his leg. He stared up at the dragon.

'Do not worry. It will come in time when you are ready. Best not to think about it.'

Jargo stretched his arms above his head and got comfortable on the ground. The faery grabbed some leaves from a bush, placed them onto the ground and sat down. The troll sat up against a large rock and poked the fire with a stick.

'I guess we should get some rest, as we need to start early in the morning.'

They all agreed and settled around the fire. The night was humid, yet a breeze blew through which kept it bearable.

The three moons moved slowly through the night skies. The shadows of the trees grew longer. The warriors shifted quietly in their sleep. Their breaths pushed out stale air. A shadowy figure lay silently under a pile of leaves, awaiting its prey. It slid itself from the pile of leaves. It grabbed a rope that was tied onto a branch high above. As it climbed to the top of the tree, it noticed a burning fire. There were a few bodies lying sleeping, which looked to be the perfect prey. It rolled up the rope into a pile next to it. It held the end of the rope tightly and leaped off the branch. It sailed into the air and waited for the rope to snap tight. The rope cracked and flicked the figure into the air. It swung with all its weight and flung itself towards the next tree-top. There was a flicker of light coming from it. The figure pulled another rolled-up rope from its back and flung it towards the tree, which cast a shadow over the campfire. The figure prepared itself once more to fly. It jumped off again and flew through the air.

Clannk shifted uncomfortably and stood up. He stretched his back and arms. He yawned out loud. In the corner of his sleepy eyes he noticed an object belting towards him.

'Yeeeeeaaaahh!' shouted the shadowy figure.

Within a split second, the troll had stood to the side and grabbed the flying figure by its neck. The rope cracked against the tree and wrapped itself around the trunk. The noise startled the others, waking them up. Kasandra wiped her eyes.

'What is going on?'

She blinked a few times to focus in the dim light. Clannk stood there, holding up what seemed to be a human. He walked over to the fire to have a better look. The others, awake now, all stood up to see what the fuss was about.

'Put me down, beast!' the figure shouted.

Clannk noticed the figure clenching a rather big knife between his teeth.

'No putting down. What are you?'

The figure hung helplessly from his neck. The troll slowly squeezed tighter.

'My name is Scabs, and I am but a mortal. Put me down before the others arrive.'

'I am Clannk, why are you here?'

'I am here because I hunt within the Slush of Kremkin. I steal from the greedy and give to myself.'

Jargo laughed and walked up to Scabs. He poked him in the chest with his wand.

'Rather admirable of you to steal from them and give to yourself.'

Scabs tried to swallow but found it difficult around the grip of the troll.

'Clannk, I think it's safe to put this mortal down.'

Clannk loosened his grip around the red neck and let him fall to the ground. The knife still remained tightly gripped between his set of dirty teeth. His face had many scars. Some of them looked fresh, while others spoke of a lifetime of injuries. He wore an oversized black cape around his shoulders. A pair of leather boots and tight black pants stuck out from under the cape.

'So where do you get all these scars from?' Jargo enquired.

'Battle scars?' Kasandra added.

'S ... sort of,' Scabs stuttered.

'Haha, I bet these scars are from your being adamant about carrying this oversized blade in your mouth.'

Grumblestumps examined Scabs closely. He walked around him in circles, raising and lowering his glasses as he passed by.

'Very good deduction indeed, Jargo. If I look closely at the shape of the scars, you will see that they are fine, almost surgical. Thus from a very sharp blade indeed. If I look closely at his blade, I notice it is very sharp.'

Scabs stood still and looked nervously at the warriors.

'In my defence, I do it because it looks more intimidating

to my prey. They see this attacker with a sharp blade flying through the air. And I do need both my hands to handle the rope.'

His hands were badly bandaged with a worn and dirty piece of cloth. They were hardened from swinging from his rope. Scabs grabbed the knife from his mouth. Jargo, anticipating trouble, waved his wand. The knife flew from his hand and into the tree nearby. Scabs looked on in shock. Jargo walked around him and waved his wand at him once more.

'Sharp edges to where they want to be,' Jargo called out.

Several knives appeared from Scabs' body: two from his boots, one from behind his cape, another from his side, and one from his arm. The wizard waved them into the tree. Kasandra went over to examine them. She pulled one out and ran her finger down the blade.

'Mmm. Sharp and shiny. This will be good at giving you a scar around your neck.'

She started casually to walk over to Scabs, pointing the knife and making slicing gestures. Grumblestumps stood in front of her and shook his head disapprovingly.

She looked down at the gnome and glared at him.

'Why must you always ruin my fun?' she asked.

Scabs grabbed his cape and opened it, showing everyone that there were no more weapons. He folded his arms and spoke.

'So, what is an unusual bunch like you doing in my Slush?'

Dekrin lowered his head towards the thief. He snorted into his face. Scabs pulled his face in displeasure.

'We are warriors representing the kingdom and we are on a quest,' the dragon explained.

'Why did the kingdom not send its knights out for this

quest? I have seen many of them pass through here in the past.'

Jargo interjected. 'I think the kingdom understands that this quest exceeds the knights' capabilities.'

'If the kingdom has entrusted this quest to the bunch of you, what is it you are in search of?'

Jargo continued.

'For one, Mother Queen has lost her marbles.'

Scabs laughed out loud.

'What? Has she finally gone loony? About time too, methinks!'

Clannk sat back down next to the fire and stoked it up with a few branches he found nearby. He scrounged around and pecked off what little flesh remained on the bones that lay on the ground.

'And why have you all got red stuff around ...'

Jargo pointed his wand into Scabs' face and ran it down the thief's cheek.

'Don't even ask,' he said menacingly.

Grumblestumps stood to the side with a slight smile on his face, and then quickly looked the other way.

'What I want to know is whether you have seen or attacked anyone who carried a satchel similar to the ones we have over here.'

Jargo asked Clannk to bring over the bags, which lay against the tree. Clannk grabbed them and brought them over. Jargo opened one slightly; the blinding light began to escape again. Scabs quickly covered his eyes with his cape until the light went away. Jargo covered up the sphere that lay hidden in the satchel.

'Was it gold that shone so brightly?'

'No. However, we are seeking someone who has one of these in their possession.'

Scab thought for a moment before he expressed a thought

in his head. He now remembered an incident that occurred earlier in the evening on the other side of the marsh.

'I do recall seeing something a little peculiar earlier on the other side, over there. I was once again high up in the trees preparing my trap for my next target when I heard a collection of giggles passing underneath me.'

Scab looked for a place to sit down and sat with one arm resting on a knee. The others found a seat and sat down next to him. Dekrin stood watch behind him.

'When I looked down through the branches, I noticed a few goblins walking and carrying a bunch of bags, much like the ones you have. I thought my luck was in, and continued to set up my trap in the hope that they might return the way they came. But they were only a few steps down the path, when a Jagged-claw Wolf appeared out of nowhere.'

Grumblestumps stood up and folded his arms.

'Jagged-claw Wolf? In these parts? Normally it only hunts on the outskirts of the Enslanted Forests of Rottingwood. There is not much prey around here. What on earth would they be seeking here?' he questioned.

'I thought much the same. However, I was more interested in what the goblins had in the bags.'

'So what did the wolf want with the goblins?' asked Jargo.

'From what I could see, they were only interested in having them for dinner. Three more wolves came out from beyond the bogs and cornered them. Before I could get any closer, one of the wolves attacked one of the goblins. To defend themselves, they threw everything they had at them, including a satchel. The satchel struck one of the wolves on its head and knocked it out. The other goblins decided to make their escape. Unfortunately, one was left behind. The big wolf grabbed this goblin by its leg and dragged him into the deeper parts of the marsh. I did notice one of the wolves sniffing at the satchel and deciding to take the bag along. I could not get there in time. It was so chaotic.'

Kasandra flipped his knife into the air and caught it. Grumblestumps made sure he was not near her in case she decided the knife could find a way into someone.

'Could you show us in the morning which way they went?' asked Jargo.

'I would gladly show you if it means I will be set free.'

Clannk grabbed the thief and took him to the tree in which his knives were still embedded. He snatched the rope that was still around the tree and tied it around the thief.

'Why am I being tied to this tree? And can you not tie me a little less tightly?'

'No,' Clannk replied.

'This is to ensure you do not go wandering off into the night without showing us which direction to take. Do not worry. There are only a few hours before it is light again,' Jargo added.

The rest of the warriors got comfortable on the ground and laid their heads down. Scabs shook his head and closed his eyes. There was not much else he could do.

'AAAAAHHH! Where are you taking me?' shouted the goblin.

'Don't you worry, goblin. I am taking you to a place in which you will enjoy being.'

'Where is that?'

'My stomach.'

The wolf continued to drag the goblin by his leg, kicking and screaming. But the goblin could not break the jaw-lock around his leg.

The three moons decided it was time for them to make space for the sun. The few birds that littered the occasional dead tree began to chirp to the sunrise. As the warm sun got up slowly, the temperature gradually increased. A bird settled into the tree where Scabs was still tied. It sat directly above him, presenting him with a gift on top of his head.

Scabs woke up with a fright. He realised what had happened.

'Oh man! Of all the trees!' he protested.

The warriors lifted their heads slowly from their slumber to see what the fuss was about. Some smiled, while others just snickered. Clannk got up and went to untie the thief. Scabs rearranged his clothing before he gathered up the rope that had tied him to the tree. Jargo kicked sand into the dead fire, making sure it would not start again.

'Right, if you are ready, please lead us to where you last saw those wolves.'

'And do I get my weapons back?' Scabs enquired.

'You will, once we get there.'

'Okay,' said Scabs. 'Please follow me down this way.'

Scabs pointed to a path littered with rocks that stuck through bits of marsh. The warriors gathered their possessions. Clannk swung the satchel and bag over his shoulder, and brought up the rear. They all hopped from one rock to the next to avoid stepping into the stinky broth that lay on either side. If they got some of the bog on their shoes, they might as well throw them away. And Jargo didn't want to be forced to get rid of his best shoes. The cloak had been his last straw.

In between two very large marshes ran a well-used path. They followed the thief eagerly. Scabs stopped in his tracks and looked around. He pointed up towards a tall dead tree.

'I was up there, looking down towards the path going in this direction.'

Kasandra knelt down and noticed drag marks and paw prints. She counted the prints carefully.

'Yup, he is right. It looks like there were four wolves. And one poor sod being dragged away. It looks like they went in this direction. I am sure I can track them from here.'

Scabs stood still and smiled. He flicked his cape to cover his body.

'Well, I have made good on my end of the bargain. Now where are my weapons?'

Jargo flicked his wand at the thief.

'Blades to where they want to be.'

The blades appeared from the air and quickly made their way into their places on Scabs' body. Scabs counted them carefully.

'It looks like they are all there,' he smiled.

'They are indeed,' agreed Grumblestumps.

'Good to make your acquaintance, but I am off to see what my traps have in store for me. Good luck on your quest.' The warriors nodded their heads.

The thief untied his rope from his shoulders and flung it towards the nearest tree. He leant back and ran quickly to pick up speed. Using his momentum, he swung from the rope and flipped himself up onto a branch. He turned and waved down to the warriors.

Clannk waved back excitedly. Dekrin, not impressed, pushed his hand down to stop waving. Kasandra continued to flutter herself along, following the marked path, while the others strolled behind. Jargo, forever watchful, had his wand out, surveying every part of the marsh. Grumblestumps continued to scrounge in his potion pouch.

The goblin was finally dragged to a halt. He lay very still, hoping they would think he was dead and leave him for good. But he figured it was a long shot. He had to try something to convince them.

'Ohhh, I am dying. This is my last word, until I keep trying.'

The goblin turned his eyes inside out and breathed out his last breath. He lay motionless until he turned blue in his face. He loudly gasped for air as he could no long keep his breath.

The big wolf looked down at the goblin and snarled.

'Nice try, but dead or alive, you taste the same.'

'No, no. This is not a go. My taste is your worst fate.'

The goblin pleaded with his rhyming words, but it did not convince the pack.

The leader of the pack spoke out.

'Throw him into the pit.'

Two of the pack wolves grabbed a leg each and dragged him to a large deep pit. They lifted him up; he dangled above the pit. The goblin stared upside down into the black hole.

'Please don't drop, for my body will go plop!'

The wolves looked at each other through the corners of their eyes and let go of his legs. The goblin sailed into the pit and fell to the bottom with a crash. A huge groan echoed out for a few seconds, then fell silent. The leader strolled over to the pit and looked down.

'Cover the pit.'

The three wolves went over to where another hole lead into the ground. They pulled out branches and leaves, and covered the hole with them. The wolves all stared at the covered pit for a while.

'So boss, when do we get to eat him?' one asked.

'Soon ... he needs to sweat a bit down there. It makes him so much more tasty and tender. There is nothing like a good tasty goblin to end the day with.'

The wolves held their snouts to the skies and howled in delight.

Dekrin stood still and listened with his face pressed up against the sky.

'Did you hear that?'

'No I did not, and I am sure no one let one go. Is your strawberry paste wearing off?' Kasandra commented.

'No, I meant did anyone hear the howling? It sounds like it came from over there.'

Dekrin pointed towards a clump of trees that seemed to be struggling to survive.

'Let me get a better view.'

Dekrin extended his wings and took flight. He did not want to fly too low, as this might alert the wolves and allow them to escape. He climbed into the sky, high enough to see over the trees. In a clearing that looked like a field of holes, he noticed a few wolves hanging around. The dragon came swooping back down to the ground and landed heavily.

'Yes, they are just beyond those trees. I do not want to fly into the field; they will surely hear me come from afar. So it is best I hang back till you have made the trip into it.'

'Good idea, dragon. I will give you a signal with a flash from my wand when it is safe to come.'

'What I suggest is that we split up and each take a corner to enter the field. This way we have a decent enough chance of surrounding the wolves without any of them trying to escape. Do whatever is necessary to stop them,' Grumblestumps explained.

The warriors agreed on the plan and began to split up. Dekrin hung back and waited patiently for Jargo's cue. Kasandra flew off to the left and entered the trees. Jargo decided to enter from the north end to make sure someone covered the top of the field. Grumblestumps entered from the right side. Clannk just continued straight, as it seemed the easiest way in. Kasandra noticed a huge web stuck between two trees. It looked fake to her. She grabbed her sword and decided to poke it. Before she could blink, the web pulled her into it. She lay firmly stuck as it wrapped her tightly into a cocoon. Her broad sword fell to the ground with a clunk. Grumblestumps climbed over a few rocks and had to swing from a few low-hanging branches to get through the maze of trees. On his last swing, he landed on the ground. His foot caught a rope hidden under a pile of leaves. The rope flung him upside down. His potion bag hit the ground, but he managed to save his glasses as they fell from his face. He hung upside down, swaying, and folded his arms in disapproval.

'Oh my,' he said.

The heat beamed down onto the marsh. The humidity sat in droplets on the warriors' skin. Clannk wiped his forehead with his arm as he walked into the trees. He pushed his way through and entered the barren field. There were several holes in the ground, looking as if they had been there for some time. They were dark and quite large at the opening, almost big enough for him to walk straight into. A large mound of hardened sand stood near the back of the field. Dry shrubbery grew intermittently between the holes and the mound. The troll stopped at one of the holes and looked in. He blinked his eyes to adjust to the lack of light. But he could not see anything.

The wolves were underground. One of the wolves sniffed something in the air.

'I think I smell lunch.'

The holes were openings to tunnels that ran underground like a maze. These tunnels protected the wolves from the intense heat of the Slush of Kremkin. It was never a good idea to hang around too long in the beating sun.

It sapped not only bodily fluids but life as well. On most days, it was sweltering. And this day was no different. Deep underground, a lair collected bones of animals unlucky enough to have become a meal. One of the black wolves ran back up to the surface through one of the tunnels. It carefully peered its head around the hole. Clannk pulled up his pants and fastened them tightly with his belt made out of rope.

'A big lunch awaits,' said the wolf quietly to itself.

The wolf snarled and growled at the troll. Clannk turned to see where the noise was coming from. He noticed a menacing wolf showing its teeth at him. But before he could say anything, several more heads popped out from different holes. He stared and counted them. He was almost surrounded by four Jagged-claw Wolves. The biggest wolf of the four stepped up towards him. It had a white stripe across its left eye. The claws were long and vicious.

'You have come to the wrong place, troll. Unless you have come for lunch. As you can see, we are all starving.'

'I am starving too,' Clannk replied.

'What do you have over your shoulder?' another wolf questioned.

Clannk pulled the bags from his shoulder and put them down in front of him.

'I have come for another like this.'

'And what makes you think we have one?' asked the big wolf.

'But Flash, we do have one in the lair,' said another.

'Why don't you just shut up!' yelled Flash.

Flash glared at the wolf with his striped eye. He rushed at the wolf and bit it on its neck. The other wolves just barked and howled until Flash let the wolf go. Clannk clapped his hands together piercingly. It stopped them and made them glare back at him.

'I am here to take back what belongs to the kingdom,' said Clannk.

'Well, I am afraid it now belongs to us. Unless, of course, you have something worth trading?'

'I don't have.'

'It is such a shame, when you could trade yourself for it.'

'I don't trade. I take.'

'You will have to fight us for it.'

From the pit, a voice shrilled out.

'Don't fight them! Please save me!' screamed the goblin.

'Who is that?'

'Oh, do not worry about him. He is just a useless goblin who will be our lunch.'

Clannk knew he had to do something, but the only thing thinking was his stomach. He knew the only thing he could trick the wolf into doing was something he was good at. Eating.

'I challenge you to see which of us can eat something the fastest.'

'My dear troll. Do you see the size of me? I am bigger than any wolf around, and I did not reach this size by howling at the three moons.'

'You find the food, and the challenge is on!'

Clannk fumbled in his pockets and pulled out little pouch which had some brindlesnaps in it.

'I will make hollow pie. First one to finish wins.'

'Hollow pie? This does not scare me.'

'It is a big pie.'

Flash pointed his claw at the troll.

'Bring it on!'

On top of the mound, Jargo's hat appeared, then the

rest of his body followed. He stood on the top and looked down at them.

Clannk waved him down and the wolves watched him carefully as he walked by. Grumblestumps still hung upside down but was determined to get out of this trap. He analysed the situation and realised that if he undid his shoe, he could simply slide his foot from the noose. He did so, and immediately fell to the ground. He picked himself up, put his shoe back on, collected his bag and headed towards Jargo.

He noticed Clannk whispering something into the wizard's ear.

'Did I miss anything?'

Jargo leaned down to Grumblestumps and explained what was happening. They both nodded at each other and stood to the side of the troll.

'They will not interfere if your wolves do not either,' Clannk said.

'To speed up the process, I will use my wand to create this hollow pie.'

Jargo waved his wand a few times and spoke.

'Hollow pie to where I want it to be.'

Two enormous pies appeared in front of them. They were so huge you could swim laps in them. Clannk looked at the wolf; it snarled back at him.

'Ready when you are.'

Clannk grabbed the first piece of the pie and began eating voraciously. Flash tucked into the pie like there was no tomorrow. Several minutes went by till things started to slow down. There was still half a pie left for each of them. But the wolf continued to eat at a frightening pace. Clannk seemed impressed, but continued to shove pieces of pie into his mouth. The other wolves looked bored and started grooming themselves. Grumblestumps whispered a few words at Jargo. They both nodded and smiled.

Clannk paused for a moment, and took a deep breath.

'I think I am full.'

The big wolf noticed and stopped eating.

'Slowing down, are you?'

Clannk sat up and grabbed another piece.

'No. No. Giving you time to catch up.'

An hour had passed and a quarter of the pie remained. Still the wolf looked comfortable enough to finish his share. Clannk sat for a moment, unsure of what to do.

'I can't anymore,' he moaned.

'Then I declare myself the winner, troll. You are mine!'

Grumblestumps stepped into the middle and raised his hand.

'If I may encourage our warrior for one last time.'

'You may, but I am sure it will not help.'

The wolf continued to eat; he was almost done. Grumblestumps grabbed a handful of pie and handed it to Clannk.

'One more mouthful and you will finish.'

'One more will make me explode!'

Grumblestumps looked very irritated and shoved the pie into this face.

'Swallow please,' he remarked.

The troll swallowed heavily and held his breath. All of a sudden, a very weird sensation came over him. It felt lightheaded, yet everything around him appeared small and insignificant. He looked down at the pie in front of him. He had one last slice left. He grabbed it and started to eat it like he hadn't eaten anything in several years.

Flash noticed him digging into the pie, swallowing pieces without chewing. He started to panic, gulping down pie and crust as quickly as possible. Within seconds, Clannk had finished his pie and started to lick his fingers one at a time.

'More. More. Tastes like more.'

With a mouth full of pie and pieces in his fur, Flash was not amused.

'How could he finish? I was almost done! This is impossible!' shouted Flash.

'Where is my bag?'

'You will get nothing! You cheated! Pack attack!'

Jargo held out his wand and flicked it at the wolves. Suddenly they were all held in the air by their tails. They whimpered in pain.

'Put us down! Just take what you want and get out of here.'

Clannk wiped his mouth and went into one of the tunnels. A few moments later, he came out with a satchel in his hand and a goblin on his shoulder.

'He might come in handy.'

Kasandra had finally managed to get a hand to her dagger and to cut herself free. She wiped some of the web from herself. Some still stuck to her hair. Her helmet hung over her shoulders, covered in web. Jargo shot a light into the sky and summoned the dragon. He flew into the field and landed next to the rest. Not far behind, Kasandra arrived.

'So what did I miss, and why are those wolves hanging by their tails?'

The dragon and the faery stood listening as Jargo explained everything.

'So in the end, it was Clannk who wolfed down the pie first?' asked Kasandra.

The warriors all laughed at the silly joke. Jargo waved his wand again and the wolves fell to the ground into a pile. The warriors walked away from the field and towards the outskirts of the marsh. They arrived at some trees that were alive and well, and took shelter in their shade.

'Let me go, for I want to know!' yelled the goblin.

Clannk held him firmly on his shoulder and refused to let him go. The faery drew her broad sword and aimed it at the goblin's head.

'What are your reasons for having these spheres? You know very well that they belong to the kingdom.'

'For gold and greed, for gold and greed!'

'You keep saying it, but there must be a reason why we are finding these spheres spread around the kingdom's cities.'

'Gold will litter, from the highest bidder!'

'So where are the others?'

'With reflection, you will get your direction.'

Kasandra looked very confused and scratched her messy hair. Jargo put his hand on the troll's shoulder.

'Put him down. I know where to go.'

Clannk lifted the goblin with one hand and flung him straight into a tree. The goblin lay against the tree, knocked out. Jargo took some time to look at everyone. They looked back.

'Wings or Wand?' he asked, with his arms folded.

They all knew what was about to happen.

Chapter 11

Glaciers of Mirror Axels

Everyone lay drifting, feeling motionless and cold.

The parts of his body untouched by water were woken by the kiss of the cold air. He listened for sounds around him, but was faced with absolute silence – a silence that for the first time felt sombre and caused shivers to run up and down his spine. There was no light; it felt as if he had been blinded for some time. All his senses felt disoriented to a point at which he could not feel any emotion. It seemed like a dream in which he was floating towards the sky. A light desperately tried to get into his head, but his mind denied all of it. The feeling was surreal, as if it was not supposed to exist. He tried to move his arms up and down. They felt numb, but as he continued to move them, a tingling sensation ran up his arms in into his neck. A cold rush of pain ran through his head; he cringed slightly. The realisation had hit that the situation was not the one he'd expected. His subconscious told his mind to open up his eyes.

Slowly he opened up one eye and saw a blue cloudless

sky above him. He turned to the side and water rushed into his face. He turned, and again his face became submerged in water. His mind fought with the concept of snapping out of it. He lowered his floating legs and stood up. Jargo was drenched head to toe. He turned around and noticed he had been floating near the edge of a huge lake. The rest of the warriors floated motionlessly in the cold water. Their bodies slowly twirled as the gentle current swept towards the shore. Their arms and legs were spread as if they were ready to be put over a fire for dinner. Grumblestumps was the first to emerge from the waters. He soon realised he had to swim to the edge of the shore where Jargo stood, wringing out his robe and hat.

The faery was next to realise where she was; she made her way onto dry land.

'Oh man, do you know how long it takes for my wings to get dry?' Kasandra moaned.

Jargo continued to wring his hat out over her head. She did not look very impressed. Derkin stood up and shook off most of the water on his body. He stomped his way out. He looked dry, as the water slipped off his leathery body easily. He flapped his wings heavily and showered the others with water. They did not look too bothered as they were already wet to the bone. Clannk eventually woke up and realised where he was. In a panic, he began to splash around frantically. Jargo noticed the troll in some trouble and shouted out towards him.

'Do you need some help?'

'I can't swim, I am drowning!' yelled Clannk.

'Use your legs!' Jargo shouted back.

'I am but I can't swim!'

Jargo saw the panic quickly taking over the troll's body.

'Use your legs!' he shouted once more.

'How?'

'Stand up!'

Clannk stood up slowly and his body rose way above the water. The water only came up to his waist. He stood very still and looked down to where the water reached. He looked back up towards the wizard and smiled sheepishly. Kasandra and Grumblestumps smiled at each other and just shook their heads. The troll slowly made his way back up to the edge of the lake. He took off his shoes and poured out a few mugfuls of lake and sand. A gust of wind ran across the lake and blew sand into the air. All of them covered their eyes until the wind dropped.

Kasandra walked up to Jargo and shoved him.

'Well done again, oh brilliant wizard!'

'A slight miscalculation on my part,' he suggested.

'Slight? Slight? Look at me, and the rest! We are cold, wet and have no cooking clue where we are!'

Clannk raised his head at the sound of the word 'cooking'. His stomach immediately grumbled again. Kasandra pointed at the troll.

'You simply can't be hungry after eating that humungous pie?'

'Yes, I thought I was full but when the gnome over there said I should finish, I became hungry again.'

Jargo pulled out his black wand and compared it to his spiral wand. With a slight flick the black wand fused a light of energy into the spiral wand. His eyes raised and stored his black wand away. The spiral wand sparked a few times, lit up like the sun, then stopped. He turned and pointed it at the faery.

'Oh, don't you dare point it at me!' she said in disapproval.

'Don't worry, I think I have fixed it this time.'

He mumbled and flicked his wand at her. She was

dry within seconds but her clothes seemed to fit her a bit too tightly. She looked down at her pants, that were now half their size, and her top, that exposed her stomach. She stood with her mouth open and raised her hands in protest. Clannk looked at the faery then quickly looked the other way, embarrassed. He fiddled with his foot in the sand.

'Let me fix this,' Jargo said hurriedly.

Another quick wave of the wand and the faery's clothes were back to normal. She ran her hands up and down her body to ensure everything was in place.

'Gee, thanks.'

Jargo turned to the others and they all shrugged their shivering shoulders. Again, within seconds they were all dry and looking as if they stepped out of a parlour.

Jargo's smile gleamed with confidence as he put his wand back.

Grumblestumps found a rock nearby and climbed on top of it.

'I would like to take a moment of your time to clear something up.'

Everyone lent their undivided attention to the gnome.

'What happened back in the Slush of Kremkin can be explained rationally. However, we must not take the threat of the Jagged-claw Wolves lightly. They are vicious creatures that roam our kingdom's cities, preying on the weak. The wolves are known to be successful at pack-hunting and stop at nothing to get what they want. However, a little bit of cunning from our side was able to outsmart them.'

'What do you mean? I beat the wolf,' said Clannk.

'You may have beaten it in an eating contest, but I must confess you had a little bit of help.'

His hand shuffled around his potion bag and pulled out some golden clover.

'Does anyone remember seeing this before?'

Dekrin looked down at the gnome's hand and nodded.

'I remember the rainbow-chaser giving it to his horse to eat.'

'Unicorn,' Kasandra corrected.

'Correct. The magical golden clover gave the unicorn the power to devour the rainbows. So, I assumed it would, in theory, do the same for the troll. When I gave him the slice of pie, I conveniently slipped some of the golden clover into the pie and shoved it into his mouth. I must congratulate Jargo on a job well done in teaching us this sleight of hand back at the Wurken Gerkin.'

Jargo stepped up and shook the gnome's hand.

'You are as sly as they come, Grumblestumps.'

Jargo just laughed and patted the gnome hard on the back. Grumblestumps looked over his glasses and tapped his nose with his finger.

'The clover made me hungry. No good,' Clannk moaned.

The faery shifted her sword and checked her daggers for sharpness. She pulled out a sharpening stone and rubbed the edges of the daggers.

'We now have three spheres. What about the rest?'

'Well, there are five in total, each one representing a part of the kingdom.'

'What did the goblin mean by "reflection will show you direction"?' Dekrin asked the wizard.

'I thought about that, and realised that he was being cryptic in goblins' usual rhyming way.'

Jargo folded his arms once again and played with his beard.

'What triggered a thought in my head was the word "reflection". In many years of serving the kingdom, I have seen places that normal beings never get to see in their lives.'

The gnome, keen to add a comment, spoke.

'What do we know that reflects?'

He looked around and noticed how the tall mountains that surrounded the lake reflected in the water. He scratched his beard unintentionally.

'Perhaps this lake reflects? Do I assume correctly that the next sphere could be hidden underwater?'

'My initial thought was to bring us to the Great Lake. But while floating in the cold, numbing water earlier, I realised that nothing really lives or breathes in this lake.'

'So if it is not the lake, what else would be able to reflect?' asked the faery.

'I am not sure, but I do have another idea. It means we would have to travel a bit again.'

Dekrin immediately stepped forward and pushed the wizard out of the way with his snout.

'The only travelling we are going to do, for now, is on my back.'

Several hands went up in approval. It seemed everyone was more eager to try the dragon than to find themselves floating in some near-freezing water again.

'So where do you suggest we travel to?' asked the gnome.

'The lake here borders the mountains that lead to the frozen zone. It's been said that this zone has remained frozen for many millennia. The mountains are separated by a canyon that is deeper and darker than the night. A huge glacier sits in this canyon and runs between these mountain tops. There are many crevasses and caves around the mountains, and some of them have been known to house a few stowaways, thieves and peddlers.'

'Let's fetch us some bad guys!' said Kasandra eagerly.

Jargo gestured to the troll to tie up the bag containing the spheres. Clannk fastened it around his shoulder with a knot, ensuring that it was secured properly by giving the rope a good yank. Dekrin lowered himself to the ground and offered his right arm for them to use as a ladder up towards his back. Jargo and the gnome pulled themselves up onto the dragon's back. Kasandra took flight and sat in front of the gnome. The troll lifted himself up with one hand and sat down behind the wizard. They happened to sit from tallest to shortest.

'I see everyone has a decent view,' said the dragon.

Approving nods went around. Hands grabbed what they could and held on for dear life as the dragon took flight. He soared into the air effortlessly and cut through the low-hanging clouds. The dragon flew high into the skies, swaying from side to side to avoid turbulence. The mountains grew smaller the higher he flew. They looked down and saw how big the lake really was. The mountains had alternating flat and spiked tops. It looked as if a huge giant had trodden footsteps across the tops. Jargo pointed out a stretch of mountains for the dragon to aim at. The dragon lowered his head and tucked in his wings, which caused him to dip and shoot through the air like an arrow.

'Set us down over there!' shouted Jargo.

The dragon weaved himself towards the mountain top. He pulled his wings and spread them as far as possible. He landed on the rocky ground with ease, then turned to the others to see if they were still hanging on. There was a shared shock across their faces.

'This is a first!' said the faery.

Grumblestumps hopped off and checked if he was still in one piece.

'In one piece and not even wet.'

'And I managed to keep my breakfast,' added Kasandra.

'Right, if everyone has finished having a go at me, you are welcome to follow me in this direction,' Jargo said.

'Where are we heading?' asked Dekrin.

'Over this cliff and towards the canyon there is a collection of caves we could go and investigate. I remember flushing out quite a few goblins from them back in the day.'

They walked down a steep decline, dodging the occasional rock that tumbled past them from above.

'Dekrin, would you mind not kicking so many rocks down?' asked Jargo.

'I cannot help it, it's my big feet. The ground is loose underfoot.'

The rocky path wound as it followed the curve of the mountain. They meandered from one side to the next. They were slowly making their way down towards the bottom of the mountain, and arrived at where the path split into two.

The wizard stared up one end of the path and then the other.

'This way, I think.'

He walked off to his right while the others stood and waited. He turned around and wondered why they were not following.

'You'd better know where you are going,' Kasandra cautioned.

Jargo pointed to a tree that stood quietly on its own.

'This tree marks underground water. And where there is underground water, there is a cave.'

The warriors proceeded on foot towards the tree. Kasandra walked with her arms folded as the air became increasingly colder. The wind started to pick up and pushed the tree from side to side. The path crossed a dry river, which separated one side of the incline from the other. The decline was trickier to walk as the ground underfoot was loose and rocky. But as they started the incline towards the tree, the ground seemed to be far more solid, as if frozen. They stopped at the tree and noticed that just behind it was an entrance to a cave. The cave echoed darkness.

'So who is going in first?' asked the dragon.

'Why don't you, since you can perhaps throw some light on the subject?' Kasandra asked sarcastically.

Dekrin anxiously peered at the wizard for him to offer an alternative. Jargo pulled out his wand and pointed it towards the cave.

'Light to where I want it to be.'

The cave instantly lit up with a blue light. The wizard ushered the warriors into the cave and followed behind. They walked slowly, allowing their eyes to adjust to the light. The cave was bigger than it appeared from outside. Dekrin could easily walk upright. Clannk eagerly walked further down into the cave. He always enjoyed exploring. The further he went into the cave, the dimmer the light became. He turned and walked back slowly, waiting for the others to catch up. His foot landed on something that cracked in half. He looked down and noticed he was standing on a ribcage. With a fright, he slipped on the bones and fell backwards. There was a sound of things falling onto the ground. It echoed through the cave and caught the others' attention. Jargo ran up to see what the commotion was. The light followed him all the way to where he noticed the troll lying on his back. They all stood and stared at the troll's clumsiness.

'Troll, do you know what you are lying in?' asked the faery.

'Uh, no. I slipped and fell on something hard.'

'You have fallen into a large pile of bones,' she said.

'Bones? Bones!' he yelled.

He scrambled to get back up to his feet. But he kept on slipping on the loose femur bones under his feet. He fell straight back into the pile. From above, a big animal skull landed on his head.

'Nice helmet,' laughed the faery.

'Too many skeletons in your closet?'

Grumblestumps laughed.

Dekrin smiled and extended a hand towards the troll. He quickly grabbed the dragon's arm and pulled himself out of the pile. He grabbed the skeletal helmet off and threw it as far as he could.

'Such a pity, you looked good in white,' the faery replied.

'I do not want to alarm anyone, but what type of animal would be storing up a huge pile of bones like this?' Grumblestumps asked.

'A hungry one?' answered Clannk.

'I think this might be a feeding cave.'

Kasandra, unsure of what a feeding cave was, asked for clarity.

'Unlike the Jagged-claw Wolves that devour their prey bones and all, there is only one species in the kingdom I know that does this.'

Jargo looked at the dragon.

Dekrin watched the others look at the wizard then back at him.

'What type of species would this be?' the dragon asked.

Everyone kept looking at him intently.

'What?'

'No! The Caves of Deelg are the only places where dragons still live. The other clans died out long ago.'

Dekrin tried to make sense of this assumption that this cave once belonged to another clan of dragons. He remembered how, when he was a young dragon, his father told how the dragons were sought out by other beings for their magical powers, how they were killed for parts that could bring their killers eternal life. He knew his father was always very protective of him, as they were the only ones left after the Tirade.

'My father would not lie to me about this!'

Jargo walked up to the dragon and put his hand on his arm.

'Maybe Barzeg has not been totally honest with you.'

Dekrin shoved the wizard's hand off his arm.

'Impossible! Why would he want to keep this a secret from me?'

While the rest contemplated the fact there could be more dragons alive, something grabbed the troll from behind. It dragged him through the pile of bones.

'Let me go!' shouted the troll.

The rest turned around in shock to see what the troll was shouting about. The troll disappeared into the darkness.

'Get down!' shouted the wizard.

Jargo grabbed Grumblestumps, who stood nearby, and threw him to the ground. They heard the rush of air building up. Within seconds, a huge ball of fire surged through the tunnel and just above everyone's head. It shot past, over the back of the dragon. Luckily for Dekrin, his skin was very resistant to flames. A huge dragon with a scar across his eye and cheek shoved its way through the flames. The troll hung helplessly from its jaws. Dekrin stood up and tried to intervene. His efforts were short-lived; he was shoved out of the way by a huge claw. Dekrin banged against the cave wall and fell to the ground. The huge, dark-red dragon took flight and disappeared over the mountains.

Jargo got up quickly and pulled up the gnome to his feet. Kasandra stood up from behind a pile of bones. She shifted her helmet back onto her head. Jargo ran out of the cave to catch a glimpse of the dragon.

'Klaw!' Jargo shouted towards the mountain tops. The others appeared from the cave and looked up at the mountains. They saw nothing but snow-covered peaks. The coldness started to edge its way into their bodies. Kasandra shivered and watched her cold breath escaping. Dekrin pulled the wizard around to face him.

'Who *was* that?'

'The dragon goes by the name of Klaw. He is the last survivor of the Red Dragons.'

'But I thought we were the only surviving clan?'

'It appears you are not, Dekrin. I believe Barzeg has a lot to explain.'

Grumblestumps wanted to know more about the Red Dragons and asked the wizard to explain.

'After the Tirade of the Fire Goblins, the kingdom gave the Red Dragons two options for siding with the goblins – be banished, or face death. I remember Klaw being the leader at the time. He accepted death as a sacrifice for the other dragons being left alone. However, I cannot remember if there were many worth dying for. But somehow he is still alive. I must admit I know as little about the situation as everyone here.'

Dekrin had a blank expression on his face. The others, unsure of what to do, just stood and stared into space, deep in thought.

'At the edge of the Glacier is a place called the Mirror Axels.'

'Of course! Why did I not think of it before!'

Grumblestumps thought about it for a second.

'Yes, a mirror reflects.'

'Then what are we waiting for?' asked Kasandra.

'Dekrin, how fast could you get us over this mountain in front of us?'

'Faster than you think!'

'Good. We need to fly over it and take a right. It will get very cold where we are going. I will create a few warm items for us.'

The wizard waved his spiral wand at Grumblestumps and the faery. They were soon covered in a warm furry coat and snow-boots. Their headgear developed a growth of fur, which helped to cover their ears. They quickly climbed onto the dragon and strapped themselves in. The flight was quick; before they could blink, they were already descending towards a frozen river. The dragon landed on the ice. It cracked slightly as both of his feet planted down.

The river ran for many miles between the mountains, from a frozen waterfall upstream. The frozen water spiked its way down to the bottom. All around them, the mountain was covered in snow with bits of rock sticking out. The river resembled a glacier, with cracks on its surface as far as the eye could see. The area looked as if it froze instantly many years ago. However, the ice appeared translucent, almost pure enough to eat.

'So where to now? Where could he have taken Clannk?' the dragon asked.

'I know he would take him back to his lair, but where this is I am not sure.'

Grumblestumps lowered himself onto his haunches and felt the ice from the frozen river. It felt coarse on his fingers. He tasted it, then spat it out and wiped his lips.

'The ice from the river seems to be old and coarse, beaten by the constant winds that blow through here.'

The faery stood nearby and frowned at the gnome.

'Which means what?' she asked with her arms folded.

The gnome got up and walked over to the frozen waterfall. He held his hand against the ice for a moment. He leant forward and stuck his tongue out.

Jargo pointed his hand out at the gnome and shouted.

'I wouldn't do that if I were you. You tongue might stick to the ice.'

The gnome ignored the advice and proceeded to lick the frozen waterfall. Kasandra couldn't bear the sight and covered her eyes with her furry coat. Dekrin started to make snowballs. Not sure what to do with them, he threw one at the faery. Kasandra felt something hit the back of her head and noticed the dragon with a handful of snow, smiling happily. He scooped up some snow and used his tail to flick the pile at the faery. She was covered up to her waist in snow, and laughed.

'Will you two stop messing around?' asked Jargo.

Grumblestumps stood very still. It made the wizard very nervous.

'See, I told you not to lick it.'

Grumblestumps waved for the wizard to come closer. He grabbed the shoulders of the gnome, ready to pull him away from the frozen waterfall. But he noticed the gnome was not stuck to the ice as he thought. The gnome asked him to come closer.

'Lick it,' he said

'What? Lick the ice?'

'Yes. Lick it.'

'I am not going to lick it.'

'Just LICK IT!'

Jargo stuck his tongue out and licked the ice with the tip of his tongue. He smacked his lips together to taste the ice from his tongue. He moved forward and licked the ice again slowly. Then he held his tongue against the ice for a few seconds.

Grumblestumps turned to the wizard and smiled.

'You notice it too.'

'I do.'

Kasandra opened her eyes and saw the two licking the ice several times.

'What on earth are the two of you doing?'

'Although the ice appears to be frozen, it is warm to the touch. Cold enough to be frozen, but not cold enough for your tongue to stick to it.'

'I think we have found our lair!' said the gnome confidently.

The faery wrapped herself tightly in her furry coat; Dekrin, baffled by what was going on, asked a question.

'What does this all mean?'

'Behind this frozen waterfall sits Klaw's lair.'

'But I thought this place had been frozen for centuries?'

'Klaw has developed a unique hiding place. No wonder your father assumed he was dead.'

'I still do not understand,' said Dekrin.

'Step back while I give us an entrance to this lair.'

Jargo whipped out his spiral wand and aimed it at the centre of the waterfall. He mouthed a few words, and a light poured out and struck the ice. It bounced off and hit a pile of snow. The pile exploded and the snow rained down. He tried once more, and the same thing happened again, but a different mound of snow was struck this time.

'This is strange. I had better use my black wand.'

He pulled the black wand from its velvet pouch and held it above his head. Again, a bright yellow light emanated from the wand, and struck the waterfall with force. A hole appeared, but as soon as it was formed, the ice around it instantly closed it up. He tried several times, but to his disappointment, he could not make the hole big enough to give them all time to make their way in. The gnome told the wizard to stop.

'The only way in is through the breath of a dragon.'

'I agree with you. It looks like your spell will not break the fierceness of the frozen zone. Yet somehow Klaw found a way through himself. This is a secret worth knowing about,' said the gnome.

'Luckily we have a dragon on our side.' the wizard added.

Kasandra, with her arms still folded into her coat, spoke.

'Have you forgotten the problem here?'

The others looked on.

'This dragon does not breathe fire!'

Dekrin interrupted the conversation with a stamp of his foot.

'Correction, I have not learnt yet.'

'I could pull my hair out!' she yelled.

Her anger caused her to grow bigger. Her coat, which once touched the ground, now only reached her knees.

'I think you are close to doing so, Dekrin. Remember earlier in the Slush of Kremkin, when you made sparks? Your body is ready. Now you need to light those sparks. Somehow, you need to find this ability. You need to find a balance between your fear of fire and your willingness to create it,' said the gnome.

Dekrin paced the ice for a while. He knew he had to do this, as he did not want to face the thought of the troll dying at the mercy of one dragon's power or at the lack of power of another.

'But how am I to balance the fear against the willingness?'

'Take it from me, when someone makes me angry, I

use the fear of resentment to my benefit. It makes me grow bigger. The more resentment, I feel the bigger I grow.'

The dragon thought about the example for a bit. It made sense to him, but it still felt difficult to put into practise.

'I know I am willing, but how do I translate the fear into some form of anger or resentment? This is something I need to practise.'

The faery started to lose patience. She knew their fellow warrior's life was at risk and there was no time to lose.

'Listen, dragon. This is not a time to think, but to act!'

'Wait. Please give me a moment to understand this!' he pleaded.

The other two just looked on at the faery, who was about to lose her cool. But before they could do anything about it, Kasandra pulled out her sword and rammed it straight into the dragon's tail. He flipped round and swung his tail viciously. An emotion ran over the dragon's face that they had never seen before. Its teeth snarled and smoke started to pour from its nostrils. The dragon's hands formed fists and the back legs stood fast. He leaned back and widened his shoulders. The dragon shouted at the faery.

'What the ...!'

Sparks began to fly out of his mouth. A gust of wind was forcing its way at her, and she dived for cover behind a pile of snow. A ball of fire burst from the dragon's mouth and hit the pile of snow. In an instant, the snow melted to reveal the faery covering her head with her arms. The wizard and the gnome stood with their mouths open. Eventually the gnome mumbled a few words.

'Oh my.'

The dragon grabbed Kasandra's sword from his tail and threw it to the ground. The faery, still hunched with her arms over her head, looked at the dragon through a gap in between her arms. She got onto all fours and then pushed herself onto her feet.

'You, you breathed fire!' she shouted in joy.

'I don't care about the fire! I want to know why you stabbed me with your sword!'

Kasandra ran and hugged the dragon around his leg. The other two ran over and patted him on his body.

'Oh wait ... I breathed fire. I BREATHED FIRE!'

Kasandra, still hugging his leg, squeezed it harder.

'Yes you did, you sure did!'

'How was this possible?' he asked.

Grumblestumps, always keen to explain, stepped back from the dragon.

'Kasandra knew you were not in a position to create your own anger or resentment. She figured it would have to come from us without your knowing it. She figured you might resent one of us if we were to hurt you in some way. Well, what a way to bring out the best in you.'

'Well, you could have warned me,' he said sheepishly.

Kasandra smiled up at the dragon and let go of his leg.

'I think you got the point.'

She picked her sword up and smashed it against the frozen river. Frozen dragon blood broke from the sword. She wiped the blade across her coat and slid it back into its sheath.

'Now that everyone has forgiven each other, I think we have a troll to save.'

Jargo stepped towards the frozen waterfall and waited for the dragon to step to his side.

'I am not sure if I can do this again.'

'I could always use my sword to speed things up, dragon.' She said.

'No, no. It will not be necessary. I am sure I could easily replicate the feeling I had about three seconds ago.'

'Such a shame, really,' she added as she patted her sword.

Dekrin took his position in front of the waterfall and spread his legs slightly. He squeezed his fists and raised his head. With one breath, he shot a fireball towards the ice. It seared straight through the frozen waterfall. The hole held its form for a few seconds then began to close up.

'Okay, everyone. Get ready to run through. I will blast off one more.'

They all lined up and waited for the dragon to do what was needed. He fired up another ball and it hurled it towards the ice. This time it melted a bigger hole, which they were all able to run through. They entered the hole with ease and stopped as they got inside. Jargo had his hands on his knees and was breathing heavily.

'I have *got* to get fit.'

They turned and watched as the hole quickly closed up. It only took a few seconds before they were sealed up inside. They examined the inside of the cave. It appeared to be made completely out of ice. Crystalline shards of reflective ice pointed in every direction. The light bounced off these mirror-like structures. Dekrin raised his arm and tapped the shards with his claw. A piece broke off and fell to the floor. Within seconds, a new shard grew in its place. It was almost as if the ice had a life of its own. The walls and surfaces of the cave stretched vastly, drawing the roof of the cave towards itself. It felt as if the top was narrower than the floor. Blocks of ice, which glowed a light blue, were packed systematically.

'Which way now?' Dekrin asked.

'The only way we *can* go, which is forward,' Jargo answered.

Dekrin took the lead and marched into the winding cave. The rest followed one by one. Grumblestumps was amazed at the sheer beauty of the ice, and kept on feeling it as he walked. Kasandra continued to hug herself in her furry coat. The cave wound to the left and then to the right. The followed until they came upon a split. The left tunnel was darker than the right.

'I suggest we split up here. I do not think I will be able to fit in there,' said Dekrin, looking at the cave to the right.

The further the right-hand tunnel went, the smaller it became. It was easily noticeable from where they had been standing. However, the left tunnel seemed to do the exact opposite.

'You go left, and the rest of us will go right. If you do not find anything significant, be sure to meet back up at this point.'

'Agreed,' the dragon said.

The wizard cautioned the other two to follow him from behind. He held out his spiral wand and slowly put one foot in front of the other. His hand balanced himself against the side of the wall. The gnome held onto his potion bag tightly and noticed a slight flickering of light ahead of them. Kasandra followed lazily. The gnome's eyes never left the mesmerising ice structures as they continued to walk. The walk into unknown territory was slow. But they all knew there was a vicious dragon lurking in the shadows. The flickering light grew bigger the closer they got. The tunnel narrowed itself so much that the wizard almost had to walk on his haunches. But it soon entered part of the cave.

They all came to a stop and looked at the immense pile of jewels and gold that glittered before them. Grumblestumps picked up a huge diamond and examined it. Kasandra stood with her mouth wide open, then smiled. She dropped the fur coat to the ground and flew herself up to the top of the pile. Jargo examined the room carefully and realised that he had seen rooms like this before. These jewel rooms were always secreted away from prying hands, and had always belonged to a dragon. These creatures loved the immense power it gave them. Trading with jewels and gold could get you just about everything. Kasandra grabbed several gold necklaces, rings and crowns, and put them on.

'Look at me! I am so beautiful!'

She flashed the jewellery on her fingers. Grumblestumps just shook his head and continued to stare at the huge diamond he had in his hand.

'Kasandra, I suggest you put all of that back where you found it. Dragons are very particular about whom they share their gold with.'

'I am sure they won't notice one or two missing pieces.'

'Let me just warn you that if any piece goes missing from here, *you* will go missing.'

Grumblestumps quickly put the diamond back where he found it. The faery dropped the rings and necklaces back on top of the pile. She flew down past the wizard. He held his hand out as she flew by, and grabbed the crown off her head.

'Oh, sorry, I forgot about that.'

'I'm sure you did,' said Jargo sarcastically, throwing the crown onto the pile.

'I guess we should go and find the dragon?'

The dragon paused as the tunnel entered a large, dark cave. It felt cold; the sound of dampness ticked onto the cave floor. He could barely make out what was inside. His eyes squinted as he tried to adjust to the darkness. He considered creating some light. He turned his head and looked up at the roof. It was high enough from the floor. The dragon breathed in, then forced out a blast of fire that ran across the ceiling to the back of the cave, lighting it up for a brief moment. The dragon blinked in the brightness. A shock of panic crossed his face as his eyes caught the shape of another dragon standing in front of him.

'Who are you?' it asked.

The cave swallowed itself with darkness.

'I am D ... Dekrin,' he said nervously.

'Why are you here? And how did you find us?'

'We came for our friend. You took him from us not so long ago. We want him back.'

'I took nothing! Get out before I decide to take your life.'

Dekrin stood still, unaware of his next move.

'Not before I get my friend back.'

Dekrin heard a very familiar sound building up. He turned his head away, knowing he was about to be blasted by dragon's breath. He covered his face with his arm and his body with his large leathery wing. The cave lit up as fire came from the dragon. It was not directed at him, however, but at many lantern-like sticks that were mounted on the wall. The fire crackled and flickered against the icy walls. Some of the ice started to drip slowly as it melted near the flames. Dekrin peered from above his arm and noticed the dragon standing before him.

'Who are you?' he asked.

'I am Sylverrise, son of Klaw and leader of the Red Dragons.'

'Son? Impossible. I thought the red dragons died out years ago? How are you even alive? My father told me we were the only ones alive.'

'Your father? Barzeg? Haha, how naïve.'

Derkin frowned.

'How do you know about my father?'

Sylverrise smirked, walked over to Dekrin and stared into his eyes. He was slightly taller and bigger than Dekrin.

His skin was a deep red, but his leathery wings were silver. Dekrin found this very unusual.

'I do not know your father. I know of him.'

'Where is my friend?'

From the back of the cave, another dragon appeared. It stood taller than any he had seen before. It was red and grey, and looked old and weary. It limped over, holding the troll with its hands. It held its huge claw across the troll's throat.

'You want your friend back?' it questioned.

Dekrin noticed it was the same dragon from earlier. It had the same scar across its face and left eye.

'Yes, release him immediately. Before my friends arrive!'

'Your friends do not pose a threat to me. I have disposed of them before and I shall do it again!' it shouted.

'Father, I shall take care of this. Go and rest.'

'Do not tell me what to do, Sylverrise. I am still strong enough to take on anyone.'

Dekrin, unsure of what was happening, walked up to Klaw. He was quickly stopped in his tracks by the younger dragon.

'Where do you think you are going?'

'Listen, Sylverrise. My quarrel is not with you. I want my friend back, and the bag he was carrying too. I am not sure what you want with him. Do you care to explain?'

Klaw shoved the troll towards Dekrin and watched him fall to his knees. Clannk got up and wiped his knees. He stepped up to Dekrin and patted him on the shoulder in appreciation. Dekrin pushed the troll behind him and ordered him to stay there.

'You can have the troll. But you will not be getting the bag back.'

'What could you possibly want with the bag?'

Sylverrise noticed some blood dripping from his father's mouth. He wiped it for him, and noticed that his legs were weakening. He gently took him to the back of the cave, and laid him down.

'Dekrin, my father is dying. Barzeg knows this and chooses to do nothing. So we have been speaking to the goblins.'

'What has my father got to do with this?' Dekrin asked.

'Your father is the only dragon alive who knows the secret of the elixir. If we do not get our hands on it soon, my father will die.'

Dekrin shuffled on the icy floor. He did not understand why his father did not tell him about the Red Dragons. Why was it so important to keep it a secret from him?

'It is very easy, Dekrin. I was willing to trade our fortune for the spheres with the goblins. Then we had something of real value to give to Barzeg for the elixir.'

'But I thought the goblins stole the spheres from the kingdom. What is it worth to them?'

Sylverrise patted his father on his head and watched him drift off to sleep. He got back up from his father and stood next to Dekrin.

'We are not here to fight, but we will fight if we have to. I will do anything to keep my father alive.'

Dekrin looked at Clannk, but the troll was too preoccupied with chasing his cold breath around the room.

'The goblins initially stole the spheres for us, but Glasshook had other ideas and told his minions to sell them one by one to the highest bidder. They were hoping to get more than what we could offer.'

'They always seem to be chanting "For Gold and Greed",' said Dekrin.

'By chasing those who had bought the spheres, we soon realised that you had been after them all along. We knew it was only a matter of time before the wizard would come for us.'

'And for you we have come,' the wizard said as he stepped into the cave.

Jargo walked up to Dekrin and pulled his black wand from his velvet pouch. He held it up menacingly at Sylverrise. The dragon stared back at the wizard and snorted cold air into his face.

'You do not scare me, wizard. We have dealt with you before. We can deal with you again. By the way, is that a new cloak?'

'Let us leave that in the past where it belongs,' the wizard said through clenched teeth.

Dekrin needed to convince the Red Dragons to give them the spheres. He had to think quickly before the wizard suggested other ideas.

'Okay, Sylverrise. Trade me the spheres and I promise you I will bring the elixir before the setting of the three moons.'

Jargo turned to Dekrin and opened his mouth. But the dragon shoved him with his tail, making the wizard fall onto his behind.

'Oh, careful, Jargo. The floor is very slippery with this ice and all.'

'How do I know I can trust you?' the Red Dragon asked.

'If you do not, you can come after us. You know where we are.'

'Deal. But you will need all five to convince Barzeg to trade.'

Kasandra stood next to Jargo and helped him up. She drew her sword and held it at the dragon. Sylverrise disappeared into the back of the cave. A sound of shuffling was heard. He returned with the bag of spheres. The troll walked up and immediately grabbed it out of his clutches. Clannk flung the bag over his shoulder and made sure, by tying several knots, that the bag would not leave his side in any hurry again. Dekrin asked the troll to check that all the spheres were there. He opened it up slightly and the blinding light struck all the corners of the cave, lighting it up like the sun on a hot summer's day. He closed his eyes and felt around in the bag. The spheres felt smooth in his bulky hands and warm to the touch. Each sphere felt different in texture and temperature. It made it easy not to count the same sphere twice.

'Um, three here,' he said, nonchalantly.

'Where is the sphere you have been holding on to?' asked Dekrin.

Sylverrise pulled another satchel from a pile of gold that lay in the corner. He threw it across to Dekrin, who caught it and handed it over to the troll. The troll checked the satchel and placed it into the big oversized bag with the rest of the spheres.

'Remember our deal, Dekrin. I know where to find you. I don't have long.'

Dekrin nodded his head and turned away towards the exit of the cave.

'One more thing. You might want to know where the last sphere is. It was mentioned that the last one was with the goblin Glasshook.'

'Why would he want to hang onto them, when it was his idea to get rid of them?' Dekrin asked.

'It is said that now that he knows how much they are worth, he went to seek out some help to create new spheres.'

'Impossible! We know it has always been just the five.

This is what keeps the kingdom in equilibrium,' said the wizard.

'True, but goblins would do anything for Gold and Greed.'

Dekrin turned to the wizard with a confused look on his scaly face. He was still not sure why anyone would go to such great lengths to replicate what cannot be replicated.

'I might have an idea where to go,' pondered Jargo.

'I will give you a hint. Go to where the golems are. There your answer will lie,' Sylverrise replied.

'Oh … that's not where I was thinking,' said the wizard sheepishly.

Grumblestumps looked up at the wizard and tugged his robe for his attention. He was excited to ask a question.

'Do we travel by wand this time?' the gnome asked.

'First, we need to find a way out of this place.'

'Why don't we just go the way we came?' asked Kasandra.

'Another good idea. Why am I not thinking of this?' asked Jargo.

'Let's go. We have lots of time to make up. Dekrin, lead the way, please.'

Sylverrise watched the warriors leave the cave. The light was dimming as the burning sticks neared their ends. He turned and walked over to his father. He put his hand onto his father's forehead and stroked it. He whispered quietly.

'I think they might have fallen for it. Let's hope he will deliver.'

Klaw looked up at his son with one eye open. He raised his arm and placed it onto his shoulder.

'Son, Barzeg's son will deliver. It is Barzeg, I am afraid, who won't.'

He pushed out an uneasy breath and closed his eye again.

The others made their way to the end of the tunnel.

'Everyone stand back, please,' he cautioned.

For a moment, it seemed he could not breathe fire. Out of the corner of his eye, he saw the faery drawing her sword. Within a second he powered up enough flame to blast straight through the ice. Jargo was first to run through the hole. It was so big that the others casually walked through it. It took several seconds to close.

'Good shot!' remarked Kasandra.

'Not bad, for my fourth try,' agreed Dekrin.

Grumblestumps tapped his nose at the dragon.

'Not bad indeed,' he said.

'Where now?' Clannk asked.

'There is only one place where the golems reign. We need to find the Rocks of Granker,' said the wizard.

'Sounds a lot warmer than this place,' grumbled the faery.

'Trust me, when you see where we are going, you will want to come straight back here,' said Jargo.

'Rocks? How bad can rocks be?'

Jargo whirled his wand and everyone instantly found themselves roped onto the dragon's back.

'Since everyone prefers to travel by air, travel by air we shall!'

Jargo pointed with his wand into the sky and the dragon took flight. They slipped into the cool air just above the tall, jagged mountains. They had never looked as beautiful from above as they did that day. It felt, for once, that there was something to look forward to.

Chapter 12

The Rocks of Granker

When it rains in the kingdom, it pours. When it pours, it stirs up the dirt into mud. When mud gets stirred up, it bears life. Then life gets up, and moulds itself into form. The form creates a body. This body goes in search of work.

The air felt hot and sticky just above the deep crevice that stretched itself into a huge hole. Lower down, in the depths of the hole, the air bounced off rocky edges. Swirls of wind caused those who looked down into it to cover their eyes.

The walls were chiselled rocks; a huge staircase spiralled all the way to the bottom. Every so often, a few rock fragments would be spat out at the top of the crevice. Tools tapped away faintly at the bottom. The deeper you looked into the chasm, the darker it became, and the more prominent the dots of red that stared back up.

Golems were hardworking beings who enjoyed the fact they gave meaning to something or someone's life. If they could work hard for you, it was worth it for them to be who they were. Golems were animated, anthropomorphised beings, created entirely from inanimate matter. They were mud-coloured with red lava-like eyes. One group of golems worked deep into the earth. They harvested anything and everything they could lay their hands on, depending on what they were instructed to dig out.

A figure stood, holding out a shape that was made of granite. He held it up to the light to see if it would reflect. His eyes stared at the object for a while before he started to turn it in his hand. The round object bounced off the palm of his hand as he made separate attempts at throwing it in the air and catching it again.

'Could someone get me more of these?' the figure asked.

Four smaller figures came from the dark, giggling. They stood neatly in a row in front of the figure. A familiar hook made out of glass pointed at them.

'NOW!'

'Yes, my Master. We will be faster,' they sang in unison.

The four stout goblins looked at each other and giggled again. Blister extended his hand and allowed Glasshook to drop the granite sphere into his hand. He held it tightly between his hands and ran off into the darkness. The other goblins skipped together as they followed.

One main spiral staircase made its way down into the dark hole. On each level, a hollowed-out cave met the staircase. A golem was seen hard at work, shovelling away in the hope to extract what goodness they could find so deep within the earth. Scattered lights lit the rocks, making the eyes of the golems even more menacing. Their eyes focused on the job at hand. The golems never tired and dug until there was nothing left to dig. But the goblins had hearts, even if their hearts were small. Glasshook felt that to maintain order within these realms, everyone needed some form of rest. A huge horn twirled down into the darkened hole. A goblin ran up the stairs to the top. He grabbed the horn at the tip and blew as hard as he could into it. A slow hollow sound echoed down into the deep darkness. This low hum rang out three times before it stopped. The golems stopped their digging and stared back out from their caves. They all walked out together and stood at the openings of their caves, their eyes all glowing red, and looked up towards the light above. The golems blinked in unison and slowly formed a single line. One by one, they made their way back up to the top. Each one dragged a huge sack up the stairs. The bags clunked together as they jolted up one step at a time. Occasionally a clunk would ring out of tune, but soon fell into step with the other sacks' monotonous song again. The golems climbed the last steps slowly and formed a circle around the mouth of the hole.

A crude wooden hut, its planks badly hammered together, stood at one end of the hole. A door big enough for a dragon swung gently in the wind. A burly goblin sat towards the back of the hut in a rough wooden chair. Two shorter goblins stood on either side of him. His hook scraped lines into one armrest. Glasshook picked his teeth with a splinter he pulled from the chair. A golem stood hunched near the door with his bag still in his hand. It blinked to adjust to the light, even though it was fading into dusk. It was not often that they got to see much sunlight. They preferred to work in the dark; it was when they worked best.

'Let them enter one by one.' Glasshook motioned with his good hand.

Pile moved over to the entrance of the doorway and pointed at the first golem in line. It slowly made its way into the hut. It stopped and stared at Glasshook with its lifeless red eyes. Blister handed Glasshook the imitation black sphere. Glasshook held it for the golem to see. It continued to blink slowly and then looked back at the goblin.

'Let me see what you have, golem,' he asked.

The golem scratched lazily in his bag and produced a very badly cut sphere. It was brown and looked like a rotten apple.

'NEXT!' Glasshook shouted.

Pile, still standing at the door, summoned the next golem into the hut. Its shoulders collided with the golem that was exiting the hut. It stood motionless with its bag to the floor and stared at the goblin. The golem scratched in its bag and produced another inferior imitation of what the goblin was looking for. One by one, the golems came and left. Their spheres did not impress the goblin. The dusk became the night, and the night grew dark, with only the light of the three moons reflecting onto the night sky. Each golem that left disappointed went back into its cave, where it stood for the night until it was put back to work by the horn. The last of the golems entered the hut with its bag. It shuffled, and pulled out a uniquely rounded red sphere.

'Hand me the sphere, golem.'

The golem placed the sphere heavily in Glasshook's hand. The sphere felt solid, yet light enough to hold in one hand.

'Good weight. Good colour. Can you get me more of these?'

The golem blinked twice. The goblin assumed that this was its way of confirming his request. The golem turned around and headed back out, down the spiral stairs. It stopped and stood still inside the cave, facing where it was supposed to dig. It blinked its eyes once, then stood with its arms at its sides.

'Where are we heading?' The dragon asked.

Jargo shifted in his seat and leant towards the dragon's ear.

'The place is not far from here, but we need to land somewhere for the night.'

'Okay, you just say where.'

Jargo pointed towards a flat plateau that glimmered in the night sky. The dragon sailed down towards a safe landing spot. His wings flapped hard as he landed softly on his feet. The warriors climbed off one by one and checked themselves to ensure they were all in one piece.

'Much better flight, thank you, Dekrin.' the gnome said appreciatively.

Jargo waved his wand and a small fire lit up. Kasandra pulled her coat closer to her body and rested her chin on her knees. Clannk lumped himself down next to her and lay on his back with his arms folded behind his head. He stared up at the sky and counted the stars. The gnome found an oversized leaf nearby and placed it on the ground. He sat down on it and laid his potion bag beside him. Jargo paced around the campfire with his arms behind his back. He surveyed the surrounding area carefully, making sure they were safe from harm.

'A sniffling for your thoughts?' Grumblestumps asked.

'This just does not make sense,' the wizard pondered.

'What does not make sense?' asked Kasandra as she lifted her head from her knees.

The wizard held his arms out wide and then slapped the sides of his legs.

'This! I mean, why have the goblins and the Red Dragons sided again after the last time?'

'As Sylverrise put it, the motives have now changed. This is something only the goblins will know,' said Dekrin.

'True, however I am pleased with everyone's team effort in attaining the four spheres so far. Now it is up to us again to find the last one and end this catastrophe.'

'Cat...cat..?' Clannk stumbled with the word.

'Catastrophe,' Kasandra corrected.

'The only stumbling block we are facing is Glasshook,' Jargo said.

'I do not think he will be very pleased to see us again,' said the gnome.

Kasandra stood up and drew her sword. She ran her finger down the sharp end of the blade and watched it flicker in the firelight.

'I think I have a friend who will be delighted to meet him.'

Jargo nodded his head in agreement.

'I agree ... we might have to use brute force this time. You can only trick a trickster once.'

The dragon stood up and smirked at the warriors.

'Luckily I have matured in the nick of time. I have a feeling it is going to be a fiery day tomorrow.'

'Make sure you all get a good night's rest. We have to approach at the crack of dawn. The goblins will be at the weakest.'

'Since they will still be drunk, yes,' Kasandra added.

'We approach at dawn. Let us be ready. The goblins have good eyesight except when it is dawn or dusk.'

The wizard removed his black wand from its velvet pouch and waved it above everyone's head. A dome appeared over them and then disappeared.

'What was that?' asked Clannk.

'I surrounded us with an invisible shield. There are some nasty bugs around here that could keep you up at night.'

A bug flew by and hit the shield. It was stopped in

its tracks by the barrier and slowly slid down onto the ground.

'Works wonders!' Kasandra said with a smile.

The warriors all settled in for a good night's sleep. Kasandra turned and closed her eyes. She had a smile on her face. She laughed at Clannk, who had fallen asleep by counting the stars. The troll lay with his arm on the ground, but his finger was still pointing.

It was deep into the night and the three moons were at their highest. A rustling of bodies was heard behind the huge wooden door of the hut. Chinks of light escaped through the gaps between the planks. A drumming sound and loads of laughter echoed into the night.

Glasshook sat in his hard wooden chair and drank from a rusty mug. The four minions were pouring wine, singing songs and bashing on a few drums that littered the floor. A huge chest sat in the corner of the hut. It had a rusty lock and key.

Blister, Pile, Shiftface and Cracker each had a drum that they were banging to a tune they knew. Each one had a turn to sing a verse of the song.

Money, money, money,
It's so funny
When you steal from the rich and poor.
Greed, greed, greed,
It's so funny,
As it makes us feel good for sure.
Gold, gold, gold,
It's so funny
Riches are our one big cure ...

They all burst out laughing and continued to bang on

the drums. Glasshook swayed his mug to the rhythm of the drums, spilling his beer on the floor. He took another sip and wiped his mouth on his arm. Blister and Pile quickly left the hut and came back with a gigantic barrel filled with fermented beer. Blister shoved five hollowed-out reeds into the barrel, and each of them began to suck the beer through a straw. The barrel emptied quickly and they proceeded to fight each other with the reeds still stuck in their mouths. The minions laughed so hard that some of the beer that was still stuck in the reeds spewed out and into their faces. Glasshook rocked his head from side to side, feeling the results of too much drinking. He fell face first onto the floor. The four minions turned and stared in shock for a moment, before bursting out laughing again, one rolling on the floor while the others bashed their fists on the ground. Cracker stopped laughing, held his hand to his mouth, and ran out of the hut. The other three each stood up against a wall and started to count down from three.

'3...2...1...GO!'

They ran towards each other and their heads collided with each other. They all fell to the floor unconscious. The night became silent for the first time. The wind started to pick up; it extinguished the light in the hut.

The morning crept up behind the plateau and set the ground alight with its rays. The sun shone down into Jargo's face. He opened one eye and surveyed the area. He slowly got up and cracked his back as he stretched. He noticed the other warriors still fast asleep on their spots. He walked away, but was abruptly stopped in his tracks.

'Ouch.'

Jargo rubbed his nose and realised that the shield he'd put up the night before was still active. He pulled out his black wand again and waved it above his head. He poked the air with his wand to ensure that the shield had vanished. He stored his wand and took a few steps towards the edge of the plateau. Looking down, he noticed a huge hole in the ground in the distance. He spotted a very tiny structure to the left of the opening that seemed to be some sort of hut. He turned and walked back to the others. Some coals still glowed. He kicked some dirt over them, sending some flying into the faery's face. She woke up immediately with an irritated expression on her face.

'If you wanted me up, a nudge and a cup of fermented brew would have been fantastic!'

'I could have done so, but what fun would that be?' Jargo replied.

Clannk raised his head and yawned out loud. Grumblestumps searched for his glasses and put them on. Dekrin flapped his wings, and stretched his back and tail. He waited for the others to sort themselves out before asking a question.

'Where to now?'

'If everyone follows me to the edge, I will explain.'

The warriors stood at the edge of the plateau, lined up from biggest to smallest. It was not intentional, but Kasandra looked back at everyone thinking that it might have been. They all seemed to be looking in the wrong direction when the wizard pointed to the big hole in the ground.

'Over there, the hole. This is where the golems are. This whole area is better known as the Rocks of Granker. The golems are good at harvesting these rocks, which are incredibly hard, and difficult to dig out. It takes patience and, most importantly, commitment. If there is one thing the golems are good at, it is patience and commitment.'

'Jargo, that is two things,' Kasandra pointed out.

'Yes, well. You understand what I mean.'

Clannk scratched his armpit and smelt his fingers.

'Why do they want these rocks?' Clannk said curiously.

'This, my dear troll, we are about to find out.'

Grumblestumps looked up at the wizard and lowered his glasses.

'What do you propose is our first line of attack?'

Jargo looked at the dragon, smiled and patted the gnome on his shoulder.

'What? Oh no. I hope you are not thinking what I am thinking?' Derkin questioned.

The dragon took flight and soon found himself standing in front of the hut. He noticed a goblin's legs sticking out the back of the hut, and went around to see what these legs were attached to. He saw a goblin lying face-down in some dirt, motionless. The dragon flicked a leg to see if it would stir; the leg fell back to the ground. He shrugged his broad shoulders and walked back to the front of the hut.

When he got there, he took a few steps back to size up the hut. He took the position he'd become familiar with over the last day or so, and spread his wings. He thought hard not to force too much fire. He took a breath and felt the fire stir within his belly. He let out a breath that shot out like a flame rather than a ball. The roof of the hut caught fire and started to burn. The smoke started to seep into the hut, between the gaps.

The drunken goblins lay still in a pile on the floor of the hut. The smoke crept inside slowly and tickled Blister's nose. He twitched his nose and rubbed it with his hand. The goblin opened up one eye and realised the roof was in flames.

'I smell smoke! This is not a joke!' he shouted.

Pile raised his head, some spit hanging from his mouth

to the floor. He pushed Shiftface awake and pointed to the roof.

'This is not a joke, I think I am about to choke!' Blister continued.

The three minions got up and stumbled around the room before they realised Glasshook was still passed out on the floor. They grabbed a limb each, and dragged him to the door. Blister kicked the door, and it swung open slowly. The smoke started to collect, making it difficult to see much of anything in front of them. They continued to haul Glasshook's body down the few steps away from the hut. Glasshook's head bounced off each step; the goblins rubbed their eyes to try to stop the tears from running. Pile coughed himself into a fit, before being silenced by a voice. They all turned around and saw a wizard pointing a wand at them.

'Perhaps I could be of assistance?' he asked.

He waved his wand once again, and a huge rushof water dropped from the air like a ton of rocks on top of them. It immediately woke up the burly goblin. He shook his head and spurted water out of his mouth.

'What? What is happening?' Glasshook shouted.

'The roof was on fire, Master, I am no liar,' Blister added.

Kasandra drew her sword and ran over to Glasshook. She ran the blade up against his neck. Clannk grabbed all three minions by the scruffs of their necks. They hung high above the ground, kicking their legs. Grumblestumps quickly took out a potion bottle from his bag and poured some liquid into a rag. He asked the troll to lower the squirming goblins for a moment. He ran the rag against their mouths, and each one drifted off to sleep immediately. Clannk glanced at them and continued to hold them above the ground.

Glasshook raised his hands above his head in surrender.

'I am not sure what you want.'

Jargo stepped up and jammed his wand into his chest.

'You know what we want, goblin.'

The goblin peered over the wizard's shoulder and noticed the troll with a large bag tied to his shoulder.

'I am sure you have what you are looking for.'

'All except one. And we know you have it. Now hand it over,' Jargo said menacingly.

'As you can see, my hands are tied at the moment. And besides, I doubt very much I have what you are looking for.'

Jargo clenched his jaw and pushed his face into the goblin's. Kasandra still held her broad sword against his throat. She flapped to the side to make way for Jargo.

'I know what you are up to. I know you are using the golems to develop imitation spheres to sell off as the real ones and make more gold than you have ever imagined. But I am here to put a stop to it.'

'You? You and this so-called army of yours? If I remember from last time, it took a whole bunch of your kind to defeat us. But the war is not over! Not by a long shot.'

Kasandra cleared her throat and pushed the goblin's chin up with her sword.

'Correction, oh handless one. We are not an army. We are warriors, warriors incorporated to save this kingdom from the likes of you.'

'Warriors? Well, you don't look like much of a warrior to me,' Glasshook said sarcastically.

Kasandra raised her sword and sliced off the tip of his left ear.

'What the ... ? Why did you just do that?' the goblin shouted.

'A little taste of what this warrior can do. Convinced yet?' she said.

'It is very simple, Glasshook. Give us what we need and we'll be moving along. You do not realise what you have done in disrupting the equilibrium of the kingdom.'

'Equilibrium? Do you even know what the word means? You took my equilibrium away by taking my hand. So, I am just taking back what should be mine!'

Jargo pushed the goblin to the ground. Glasshook fell onto his behind.

'If you are so magical, why do you not use your powers to find what you are looking for?'

'It is not as easy as you think. The spheres work in their own special way, a way you will never understand.'

'I think I know much more than you think,' Glasshook added. 'You can search if you want, but you will not find it with me.'

Jargo stepped over the goblin and waved his wand at the hut. The smoke dissipated, allowing him to have a good look inside. He searched the hut and found nothing. Dekrin noticed that the goblin whose legs he saw behind the hut had disappeared. He walked over to investigate. For a few hundred feet, he saw tracks on the ground – footprints, and drag marks. He took flight to get a better view of the area. He quickly saw a skinny goblin struggling to drag a very heavy, rusted chest. The dragon swooped onto him quickly and grabbed him in his jaws. He grabbed the chest with his arm and raced back towards the others.

'Glasshook! You have one chance to tell me where the last sphere is. Or this will be your last day in the kingdom.'

'If you did not find it in the hut, then I am afraid you will never find it.'

Dekrin landed near the hut, the dust swirling in the force of his flapping wings. The warriors quickly saw the goblin dangling from his gigantic jaws. The dragon threw the rusty chest onto the floor. The chest fell and lay on its side. Glasshook stood up and looked at it in horror.

'Where did this come from?' he said nervously.

'A little friend flew it here for you,' Dekrin replied.

Grumblestumps went over to the chest and tried to turn the key. The lock was rusted shut. He scratched inside his potion bag and pulled out a bottle whose label read *Grease monkey*. He opened the jar and wiped some black paste onto the lock and key. The grease made its way into the crevices and holes of the lock. The key slowly turned by itself, unlocking the chest. The grease then formed itself into a miniature monkey. Grumblestumps grabbed the black monkey, moulded it back into the bottle, and stored it back in his bag. Everyone looked at him in disbelief. He looked back at everyone, and shrugged his shoulders.

Kasandra prised open the lid with her sword. A blinding light burst from the chest. They covered their eyes with their hands. She quickly closed the chest again and the light disappeared. Grumblestumps closed the lock once more.

'Clannk, put it with the others, please,' Jargo requested.

The troll took the bag, unlocked the chest and quickly threw the spheres together. He closed the chest and started to tie a bulky rope around it. The rope made a loop, which he flung around both of his shoulders so that the chest sat comfortably on his back.

The ground started to shake violently and cracks started to appear. Panic started to fill everyone's faces.

'What is happening?' shouted Kasandra nervously.

'The kingdom is reacting violently to the spheres being thrown together!' commented Grumblestumps.

He scratched again in his bag, and pulled out the glass hook with the words *Four carries Five* written on it. He showed it to everyone standing there. But before they could question Glasshook, he was nowhere to be seen.

'Glasshook has run. I need to go after him!' Jargo said, irritated.

'Now is not the time, Jargo. We have to get these spheres back to their rightful place immediately.'

'Did I do wrong?' Clannked asked.

'No, you did perfectly,' Grumblestumps said reassuringly.

'I remember now, we have to get these spheres back before the setting of the three moons, and last night they were at their highest. We do not have any time to waste,' he added.

'So where do you propose we go?' Jargo asked.

'To the castle! Post haste!' Grumblestumps said quickly. 'I have an idea of how we can save the kingdom, the queen's marbles and ourselves.'

Kasandra sheathed her sword and put her arm around the gnome.

'Then what are we waiting for?'

'As much as I do not want to, we are waiting for Jargo.'

Jargo stared back at the gnome then back at the others. He was not sure if he was thinking along the same lines as they were.

'Places to where we want to be?' he asked hesitantly.

'Maybe a good time not to think too much about it and just to do it,' Kasandra suggested.

Jargo pulled out his wand and pointed it at the warriors.

'Hold onto your hats, everyone!' Grumblestumps said excitedly.

A flash shot from the wizard's wand, and they disappeared into the morning skies. The horn rang out into the hole and the golems began to work immediately. The air filled with the sounds of digging and grunting.

Chapter 13

The Room

The night was peaceful. The crickets rubbing their legs together made soft chirps. The sky was riddled with bright stars and the three moons shone brightly. The evening had settled in and the night wildlife was at its best. Many creatures scuffled in the bushes, looking for their daily meal. The forest outside the castle walls chatted as the breeze swept through the swinging treetops.

Cedric sat in a chair with his head back against the wall and snored his head off. His hand clutched the tall spear he used to guard the gate. The huge chained gates stood still, watching over the castle. The moonlight reflected in the fountain and the water rippled as each drop fell. The courtyard displayed itself neatly in the glimmering light; everything was in its place. The stairs up to the castle did not look as intimidating as they did in the daylight. The castle stood tall above everything else, and everything else did not seem to mind.

Deep inside the castle, near the top of the tower, sat

the king and queen's bedroom. The tower stairs led up to a door that opened onto a spacious and well-kept bedroom. A magnificent oversized bed stood at the back of the room. To the left, a huge wardrobe was stationed against the wall, and to the right sat an elegant dressing table with a curved mirror. A bay window across from the bed let the moonlight trickle in for a nightcap. King Sorbus and the queen slept soundly. His majesty slept on his side, on the right of the bed. The queen slept on the left side and left a big gap in the middle – King Sorbus enjoyed the occasional flaying of the arms during the night. It was best for her to avoid a punishment when there was no call for it. They both wore evening crowns to bed, small enough to be comfortable and safe enough not to stab their bedfellow's eye out. A velvet robe hugged each of their bodies. The night was cool, so a duck-down duvet covered them for warmth. The duvet lay light and soft above them. It looked like they were sleeping under the night-clouds. Their shoes were at their bedside, neatly placed next to each other. King Sorbus snored loudly and vibrated the duvet off his face.

In the corner of the room, the light started to swirl clockwise, more and more persistently. A whirring sound barely broke the silence and then suddenly stopped. For a brief second, the room carried on as normal.

BANG!

Out of nowhere, the dragon appeared. He crouched, as he barely fitted into the room. His whole body stretched across the window and blocked out most of the evening light. He blinked his eyes to adjust to the darkness, then realised he was in someone's room. He froze, with his wings spread against the wall and his body pushed up against the window. A few more bangs went off in the room. Some of the noises sounded muffled. The queen stirred in bed and sighed out loud. Still asleep, she turned over and put her arms around a body in the bed.

She rubbed its tummy a few times. The body started to giggle in a deep, gruff voice. The queen slowly opened her eyes and noticed a huge frame lying in bed next to her. She felt the body again to make sure it was King Sorbus. Not feeling the velvet robe, she became a little concerned.

'Sorbus?' she whispered.

King Sorbus grunted in his sleep and turned over.

'Am I snoring again, mother?' he mumbled.

He put his arm around the body next to him. He too rubbed its stomach a few times. It felt different, as if the queen had put on weight. A lot of weight.

'SORBUS?' she said more sternly.

He opened his eyes and looked at what he was rubbing. His eyes grew bigger and his mouth dropped open. They both sat up in bed as if they had sat on a pin prick. Clannk, lying in the middle of the bed, lay giggling. He smiled back at them and proceeded to give them a hearty hug. They both screamed.

'Duh, hello, Your Majesty,' Clannk said gleefully.

They continued to scream. Their heads spun around the room and noticed a huge evil-looking creature stuck against the window. They looked at each other in horror, gasped for breath and screamed again. Louder.

Clannk sat up in the bed and put his big hands over their mouths. The screams became muffled. Footsteps ran up the stairs to the bedroom. The door handle shook and rattled as a hand tried to get the door open. A shout came from outside the door.

'Unlock and open!' the voice bellowed.

The door unlocked itself and swung open, hitting the adjacent wall. Jargo ran in with his spiral wand pointed in the direction of the bed.

'Light up the night!' he summoned.

The bedroom instantly illuminated with floating candles around the room. He quickly surveyed the room to see what was attacking the king and queen. He soon noticed Clannk holding their mouths with his hand while the dragon still stood up against the wall and window. Dekrin shrugged his shoulders at the wizard.

'What? What is going on here?' he asked.

A muffled attempt at answering the wizard's question seeped through the troll's hand.

'Clannk, please unhand the king and queen,' Jargo asked nicely.

The troll let go of the king and queen and sat back up against the bed frame. The king and queen quickly jumped out of the bed and hid themselves behind the wizard.

The queen pointed at the dragon with a shaky finger.

'What is that doing in here?'

King Sorbus turned and did the same to the troll.

'And what is that doing in my bed?'

Jargo turned at them and raised his hands up slightly.

'Well, a miscalculation on my part, I guess,' he confessed.

'A miscalculation?' the queen asked in shock.

'Yes, well, I could explain,' he replied.

A shuffling sound emanated from the oversized wardrobe. It was followed by a couple of bumps, groans and moans; finally, a pile of clothes fell through the doors. The pile lay on the floor and then acquired a life of its own. It started to bear shapes – first some arms, then legs – and then stood up. Everyone in the room stared at the clothes coming to life. Jargo kept his wand pointed at the clothes. A head suddenly popped out from a long, silky, red robe.

'Grumblestumps?' Jargo said, unconvinced.

The gnome noticed the king and queen standing behind

the wizard. He bowed and shifted his glasses back up his nose.

'Good evening to the both of you,' he said politely.

'Then where is ... ?' asked Jargo.

From the corner of the room, the elegant dressing table began to shake. One of the drawers started to slide itself open. The drawer slid all the way, then fell to the floor. The faery stood up from the drawer, shook her body and stretched her back.

'Boy, you do *not* want to be caught in one of those,' she griped.

Jargo counted everyone in the room, but he still looked confused.

Kasandra walked up to the gnome and felt the silky robe between her fingers.

'This colour suits you.'

She knelt down and picked up a crown from the floor. She tried it on but it was too big for her. She nonchalantly placed it on the gnome's head and patted his shoulder. Clannk lay with his back on the bed and realised he was the only one in it. He spread his legs and arms, making snow angels on top of the white duck-down duvet.

'Would you mind not doing that?' Jargo asked the troll.

Clannk stopped and lay on his side resting his head on his hand. His other hand played with the duvet quietly.

'Is it safe for me to come away from the window now?' asked Dekrin, still stuck against it.

The queen waved her hand menacingly at the dragon.

'Make sure you do not break anything, like you did last time.'

'Yes, Ma'am.'

He lowered his head and looked down at the floor, watching his foot shuffle from side to side.

King Sorbus rearranged his crown on his head and adjusted his robe.

'So, how did you find yourselves in our chambers?'

Jargo stepped back and folded his arms.

'We successfully found all five spheres and I knew it was imperative to bring them back to the castle as soon as possible. There had already been a shift in the kingdom's axis, which we felt in the Rocks of Granker.'

'Aah, this is good news and not-so-good news. Where are the spheres right now?' replied King Sorbus.

'But how did you manage to find yourselves in here?' asked the queen a second time.

'Oh yes, I knew we had to get the spheres back as soon as possible, so I used my travelling spell and asked it to bring us to where you were.'

Kasandra leant over to the king and punched him in the leg with her elbow. She held her hand to her mouth and mumbled, 'Not much of a spell to be honest.'

Jargo forcefully cleared his throat and replied, 'It got us here in one piece, did it not?'

Grumblestumps tried to get himself out of the robe but soon found his head was stuck through a sleeve.

'The question we must answer is, where are the spheres?' Grumblestumps added.

Jargo looked at the troll still lying on his side in the bed.

'Clannk, the last time I saw you, it was neatly strapped onto your back.'

Clannk looked down on his chest and noticed the rope was still tied.

'Yes, it must still be there.'

He climbed off the bed and tried to see if the chest was tied to his back. He turned in circles trying to find it. He became dizzy and fell to the floor.

Kasandra shook her head at the troll in disapproval. Jargo walked up to the bed and shoved the pillows and duvet around in search of the chest. Kasandra grabbed her sword and started to slice up the duvet in the hope of retrieving the chest first. Feathers flew up into the air and littered the floor.

'No need, Kasandra,' Grumblestumps said and grabbed her arm.

'Well, it's not in there,' she replied.

Jargo raised his hand and flicked his wand in the direction of the bed.

'Show yourself into the light.'

The chest appeared from under the bed. It slid across the marbled floor and stopped against Jargo's legs. He bent down and unlocked the chest with the rusty key. It opened up easily and he raised the lid slowly. The blinding light shone out once more and lit up the room even more. Everyone in the room covered their eyes.

'Why do they shine so brightly?' Dekrin asked.

King Sorbus put his hand on the chest and tapped the top of the lid.

'The spheres, as you all know, are unique to the kingdom. But the light is an intriguing one. Individually they shine, but together they absorb light. If they are where they are supposed to be kept, you will find the room a very dark place. Nothing escapes the darkness. But as individual spheres they reflect light. So now you understand why most of these spheres were split, and had to be carried in a bag or satchel that could be tied up completely.'

The queen sat down on the edge of the bed near King Sorbus. Clannk climbed off the bed and walked over to the dragon. Kasandra helped the gnome out of the red robe.

'King Sorbus, why is the Kingdom shifting on its axis?' asked Dekrin.

'Well, dragon, if the spheres are taken from their place for too long, the equilibrium of our world starts to fall apart. We rely on the spheres to keep everything in order.'

'Why are there five spheres?' Kasandra asked.

'Each sphere represents a part of the kingdom in which we find sanctuary. Without the qualities that the spheres represent, we as beings cannot survive in this world.'

'And those would be?' Kasandra questioned.

'Peace, happiness, friendship, patience and love.'

Clannk licked his lips again and spoke.

'Piece, mmm. I like a piece of pie.'

'Forgive the troll, Your Majesty. He thinks with his belly and not his brain,' Grumblestumps commented.

'The troll has a brain?' Kasandra said, surprised.

King Sorbus smiled and stood up. He walked over to the bed and put his arm around the queen.

'These spheres have more influence over what we do than you think.'

'How do you mean, King Sorbus?' Jargo asked.

'Well, for instance, troll, how did you acquire your sphere?'

'How do you know he acquired one at all?' Kasandra questioned.

'Each sphere will choose a being worthy of rescuing it. It is the will of the sphere.'

Jargo looked a bit perplexed. He always understood that the spheres ensured stability of this land, but had never realised that each one could be influenced by those who surrounded it.

'I won the sphere by eating pie,' Clannk said.

'Exactly, the sphere you represented was Peace. I am sure you enjoyed your last piece of pie.'

'Lucky guess, and very convenient. But what about

mine? I won mine fair and square in a duel against the finest fighter in the land,' Kasandra said.

'Did you have to prove this to anyone?'

'I did it for my father, as he never saw me as anything. I wanted to prove to him I could be just like him, even if I was his only child.'

'And did this make you happy?' the king replied.

'Hell, yes!'

The king smiled broadly at the faery.

'You acquired the sphere of happiness.'

'Oh,' she said foolishly.

'And you, dragon?'

'My quest is not done yet with the sphere. I have to convince my father to help the Red Dragons.'

'And why do you need to do this?'

'My father loves me and wants to ensure our existence.'

'Exactly. Your sphere was love.'

A sense of coincidence quickly turned to a feeling of truth. These spheres had guided the warriors into believing in themselves and in each other to fulfil the kingdom's wishes. They were chosen not because it was convenient, but because they were the ones who needed to fulfil their destinies.

'And you, Grumblestumps? Did you happen to heal anyone?'

'I did fool someone into thinking they were healed.'

'The sphere of patience prevailed. Even though somehow tongue in cheek. A patient you healed, but nonetheless, I am sure your patient had been waiting a very long time to be healed.'

'Indeed, he had,' Grumblestumps remarked.

'What about you, Jargo?'

'I fooled the ogre, Brok, into giving me the sphere.'

'Brok? Did he not want to rip your head off?'

'Actually, he did not.'

'Then you must have made a friend. Hence, you acquired the sphere of friendship.'

The queen walked over to the dressing table. She bent and picked up the draw, then placed it back in its slot. She adjusted her hair in the mirror.

'The spheres are magnificent in their own way. Let it be known now why it was so important to return my marbles. Could you all please accompany me to restore these spheres to their rightful place?'

Jargo waved to Clannk to carry the case for them. Clannk grabbed the case and tied it onto his back. The rope holding the chest crossed his body.

'Please follow me.'

They left the chambers through a very large door. The dragon squeezed himself through uncomfortably. A staircase spiralled down a narrow tower. Each step was taken carefully as it was a steep drop to the bottom. They reached another doorway where two tall guards with huge spears stood. The door had many heavy bolts on each side. Their faces looked on.

'Guards, as you were,' King Sorbus greeted.

Both guards slightly nodded their heads towards the king and continued to stare out in front of them. They wore full suits of armour. The suits were so shiny that the warriors could see their own distorted reflections.

'Please allow us to pass,' the king asked.

'Password, Your Majesty,' one of the guards said clearly.

'The password is confirmatory.'

The guards both deposited their spears into the corner of the walls. They grabbed a bolt each and proceeded to slide them one by one. They went through ten bolts each before placing both hands onto a metal wheel. The wheels turned and squealed as they unlocked the door. The door led into a room brightly lit by the moonlight. The warriors observed the room filled with plant life, flowing water and everything nature had to offer. They were amazed that such a room could exist.

'What is this room?' Kasandra asked.

The king put his arms out and welcomed everyone inside.

'Welcome to the Benevolent Room.'

As always, Clannk struggled to pronounce the word. Kasandra glared at the troll.

'What is a Benevolent Room?' the dragon asked.

'This is the room that gives the spheres its sanctuary. As you can see, the spheres give life to everything. And everything in this room, including the kingdom, has been given life by the five spheres.'

The queen walked over to where she saw some of the plant life withering.

'As you can see we need to place the spheres in their rightful place. The room is beginning to die. And soon the kingdom will too.'

King Sorbus carried on with his explanation.

'The spheres do good, or give aid to others, selflessly, without concern for what they get in return. They are willing to give and share unstintingly.'

Jargo thought to himself how the spheres would actually have been useless for the goblins. But he knew they did not understand the true meaning of the spheres. Their judgement had always been clouded by gold and greed.

'Clannk, if you could place the chest down over there.'

Clannk untied the chest from his back and lowered it gently to the ground. King Sorbus cautioned everyone to stand back and close their eyes. He opened up the chest and removed all the spheres from their bags and satchels. The bright light bounced off the flowing water. A majestic fountain flowed gently and water fell from the top. The king placed the spheres next to each other, but this did not stop them from shining brightly.

'Something is wrong here,' the king said.

He closed the chest again and everyone opened their eyes.

'What is the problem?' Jargo asked.

'They are all together, yet they continue to reflect light.'

'Maybe we need to place them one by one into their rightful places. Where are these places?'

'They always hovered in a circle around the fountain. Perhaps if we place them in there, it might help,' the king suggested.

Jargo grabbed a sphere out of the chest and felt his way to the fountain. He dropped it into the water, but the light continued to burst out. He took the sphere again and shoved it back into the chest. Grumblestumps fumbled in his bag and pulled out the glass hook he had found many days ago. He read the message written on it aloud.

'Four carries Five.'

A puzzled look went around the room. They were not sure what it meant, but the gnome seemed to have an idea.

'Yes, I completely understand now. Why did I not think of this earlier?'

'Please explain,' the king urged.

'Bear with me for a moment. I always wondered how the goblins managed to retrieve these spheres from the Benevolent Room. They would have been blinded if they took them one by one. But this explains it all. There were four minions, and they knew they had to carry all five of these spheres out. So how can four beings carry five spheres? The numbers do not add up.'

'Do you have an idea, gnome?' Kasandra said inquisitively.

'I do, but I need hands that had influence in obtaining these spheres. I need everyone to please grab a sphere, but before you do we have to ensure one thing.'

'Which is what?' Kasandra said impatiently.

'That you follow my instructions. First, we all need to circle the chest and make sure we can touch hands. Next, when I call your name, grab a sphere from the chest and hold it out in front of you. Make sure your sphere touches the one next to you. This will form a base for the final sphere. Dekrin, being the tallest here, will place the last sphere onto the centre of the four touching spheres. This should, in theory, balance perfectly. Each sphere should absorb the light from the others in this position, rather than reflecting it individually.'

'It makes perfect sense,' Jargo said, impressed.

'I hope everyone is ready. I will take the first sphere; Kasandra, you will go next, followed by Clannk, and then Jargo. Dekrin, you know what to do next.'

The dragon nodded excitedly and took his place.

The king and queen held each other tightly and closed their eyes. Grumblestumps opened the chest, grabbed the first sphere and held it out. The rest followed one by one, holding their spheres as still as possible. Each sphere touched and sparked with a blue light. The light emanating from each one started to dim slightly. Dekrin felt his way inside the chest and grabbed the last one. He fumbled his way with his other hand over the troll's head and slowly held the sphere in its place, not wanting to let it go.

'Do you think it is safe to let go?' the dragon said nervously.

'Yes.'

The dragon let go and the sphere clinked into place. The sparks flew and swirled and the light instantly disappeared. Everyone in the room opened an eye to steal a glimpse at the balancing spheres.

'Well done! It worked!' Jargo shouted in joy.

'Now what do we do?' asked Kasandra.

'Now we slowly place it onto the fountain. There is a base on which it needs to be placed.'

The warriors moved towards the fountain, but before they could position the spheres, they started to shake furiously. One by one, the spheres flew towards the fountain and circled it in a continuous motion. They whirled around and the water started to flow powerfully. King Sorbus was not sure what was happening, but the plants that had started to wither had become green and healthy.

'Look, it's repairing the room. You have done it, warriors!' the queen said, impressed.

A huge sigh of relief went through the room. A round of high fives met each other in triumph. The room quickly started to lose all light, then became pitch black. Everyone stood very still, frightened. Jargo felt a tug against his robe.

'Was that supposed to happen?' Kasandra said nervously.

The warriors stood speechless, until Grumblestumps opened his mouth to mumble.

'Oh dear.'